AVALANCHE

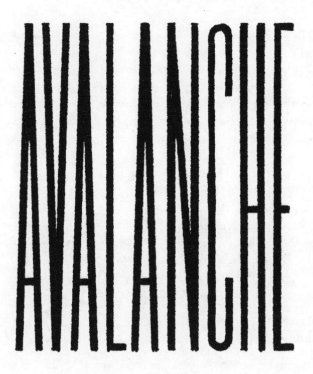

Jessica Westhead

Invisible Publishing
Halifax & Toronto

Library and Archives Canada Cataloguing in Publication
Title: Avalanche / by Jessica Westhead.
Names: Westhead, Jessica, 1974- author.
Description: First edition.
Identifiers: Canadiana (print) 2023017583X
             Canadiana (ebook) 20230175848
             ISBN 9781778430268 (softcover)
             ISBN 9781778430275 (HTML)

Subjects: LCGFT: Short stories.
Classification: LCC PS8645.E85 A95 2023 | DDC C813/.6—dc23

Edited by Bryan Ibeas
Cover and interior design by Megan Fildes | Typeset in Laurentian
With thanks to type designer Rod McDonald

Invisible Publishing is committed to protecting our natural environment. As part of our efforts, both the cover and interior of this book are printed on acid-free 100% post-consumer recycled fibres.

Printed and bound in Canada.

Invisible Publishing | Halifax & Toronto
www.invisiblepublishing.com

Published with the generous assistance of the Canada Council for the Arts, the Ontario Arts Council, and the Government of Canada.

   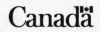

CONTENT WARNING

These stories are about white people committing acts of overt and covert racism, and systemic white supremacy. "Swimming Lesson" contains a reference to child sexual assault. "The Meeting" and "Avalanche" contain references to emotional and sexual domestic violence.

THIS IS THE WAY

YOU HAVE TO DO IT LIKE THIS. But this is the way you have to do it.

Then you need to put the special stamp on it. Don't forget that part. We have the special stamp, but you have to ask us for it. You need to submit your stamp request at a precise but unspecified moment in the process, and if you miss that moment, we are not responsible for what might happen as a result.

You have requested some additional clarification from us and we are happy to provide that here, but please pay close attention because we will not be this happy if we are asked to provide it again.

If further clarification is requested, we will tell you about the other way. That way is more complicated, but that's the way you'll have to do it if you don't take our advice about doing it the first way, exactly the way it's supposed to be done.

To be clear: we have the special stamp and we are fully prepared to give it to you, but you need to ask us for the right colour, or the stamp must remain in the drawer. We're sorry, but our hands are tied. Because of the rules. The rules apply to all of us.

If you tell us in advance that you require two stamps, we will make a note of that. But we will only make a note of it once, so you should not ask us again. We need you to understand that part. That part is very important. One note from us and two stamps for you. Remember that, or you might as well rip up your application and start over. Although you can only apply once, so starting over is not an option.

You need to change your way of doing things because it is too collaborative. There are too many people involved in your project and we don't know what they're all doing. They could be doing things we don't approve of. They could be using their own stamps! That would be one of the worst possible things. But we think you know that already. If there is an unregulated stamp that you have not disclosed to us, there needs to be a line item about it.

If you insist on involving co-applicants, then we will insist that you ensure that the names of your co-applicants are spelled correctly. We are pretty sure that the current spellings are incorrect because we are using the most updated version of Word and there was a squiggly red line under every single one of the names, including yours. There is never a squiggly red line under our name. Because we always spell it correctly.

We are supportive of the potential of your project, as we have stated. As we have stated many times. We will indicate our support often and enthusiastically. It's a good project. We plan on supporting it. But we need to support it in the way that is correct.

If you need our signature, just ask. The signature is not the same as the stamp, as we have already explained to you when we cited B. Reg. 1002/46. That was the part about the signature not being the same as the stamp.

We will say it again: the project is good. It will be good and beneficial for all involved. We are supportive of the end goal of helping you get this project done. But only if it is in alignment with all of our policies.

We will not say anything bad about the project. But the way you are doing things, that is the problem. The way you are doing things is not in alignment. As we have explained. As we have explained very clearly and outlined in the document we gave you with next steps and recommendations and then you came to us and said, "What?" And we said, "It's all there." And you got a look on your face that

4

communicated something we did not understand, so we sent you the document again.

If you lose either version of the document we provided to you, we can't be held responsible for your mismanagement. Because just a reminder: the rules apply to everyone. At our workplace, for example, we are required to complete certain mandatory courses, with no exceptions. This was not a requirement before, but now it is.

The project you are doing is good, as we have previously stated, but the goodness does not extend to you. That is quite likely the heart of the matter here, which no one is talking about even as that heart is beating out its insistent and undeniable thumping rhythm in the background. The goodness of the project stands alone, without you. If you forget that part, we will remind you.

We are supportive of this project that addresses important themes. We cannot officially give you our support in writing on official letterhead until you get the stamps in the right order and in the right colours and you do those other things in the ways we have outlined. But we absolutely agree that the themes of the project are important and necessary. We all feel very positively about those themes and what they represent, both now and in the past, and also in the future, if people keep believing that these themes are important.

But you should know that even if your project didn't exist, there would be other projects to address those themes. Because those themes are becoming more common now, which is of course a good thing. We can all agree there's no getting around the importance of those themes. If there was, we would not be having this discussion!

Things used to be easier, but even in those carefree days, the rules were in place for a reason. And that reason is: So we can all agree. So we can all have the same standard applied across the board. So there is no special treatment, which no one should receive. This is why we need the rules.

Don't worry. We will talk you through them. We think you might even come to love them as much as we do, if you keep an open mind.

Something else we are curious about is why you are interested in doing this project.

Yes, we know the themes are important. But who are the stakeholders? Please prepare a deck of the stakeholders. If you don't know what a deck is, we can't help you.

We acknowledge your frustration.

We are frustrated too.

We took the mandatory courses with the understanding that we would gain knowledge from them, but the people who came to our workplace to teach the courses expected us to know certain things in advance, and we didn't. As a result, we were embarrassed in front of some of our co-workers, and the next time we saw those co-workers at the photocopier, they smiled at us but their smile was different from the last time they smiled at us, before we took those courses.

So! Who are the stakeholders? Break it down for us. This breakdown should be comprehensive and fulsome and by this we mean it should comprise everything. Use Power-Point. Or don't. It's up to you. But we do like PowerPoint. Google Slides are fine too. Except we like the functionality of PowerPoint better. There's a thrilling feeling of momentum and anticipation that builds during a PowerPoint presentation in a way that is absent from a Google Slides presentation. But whatever works best for you.

While you're at it, please familiarize yourself with Q. Reg. 893/1B, which can be found by accessing the database we alluded to in an earlier email, via the password and username we provided in that email. Although by now that password may have expired, in which case you will need to apply for a new password within the next 30 days or no dice.

Include a clear timeline and specific outcomes. Will the outcomes clearly reflect the important themes, and will those outcomes be clearly executed in a manner that is clearly aligned with our policies, procedures, and regulations, namely L. Reg. 12/77-C, which we are bound to uphold by the rules that are in place to uphold us?

You should also be aware that we do not make the rules. The rules exist as living, breathing entities that dictate what we can and cannot do. This might sound improbable, but believe us, it's true and it's reality. And this improbable but definitely true reality can sometimes unfortunately result in awkward situations such as this one, in which we have to explain to you that we cannot change the rules because the rules have all the power. The rules tell us what to do and we have to obey the rules, even if we might occasionally disagree with the new and unwelcome direction some rules appear to be taking at this particular moment in time. Because otherwise nothing would make sense, and we're sure you can understand that!

We will say it again: we admire your passion and commitment to this project. Passion and commitment are good things that are worthy of admiration.

And so is this wonderful time of year! We hope you've been enjoying these last fleeting days of autumn. We went for a walk this afternoon and the colours were truly stunning. But mostly we were entranced by the leaves. They were drifting down all around us and crunching under our feet, and we felt quite whimsical. The weather has been glorious and we'll be soaking up the golden sunshine this weekend on our deck, which is not the same thing as the deck you'll be preparing for us, but that's the only hint we'll give you!

Once again, we will enthusiastically echo everyone's sentiments about the themes of your project being important and necessary. So please ensure that you submit everything in accordance with the way that you need to submit it, or else it will be invalidated and we can't read it, sorry.

Because, as we have mentioned, we are bound by certain regulations. And so are you.

HOW WE CHALLENGE OURSELVES

I AM DOING SOMETHING IMPORTANT and it means something. Even if you don't think so. Tomorrow will be monumental and transcendent. I know this deep in my heart and I'm feeling pumped. So I'm trying to relax and enjoy myself before it happens.

But all I can think about is your stupid article.

I wish I'd never read it, but I did, because my friend Andy sent it to me, and Andy usually sends me great articles to read. But not this time.

You know what, though? I don't care. I'm here in Mont Tremblant with my wife and my boys and we're having a blast. We arrived yesterday and the sun was shining when we checked in. Our hotel is halfway up the hill, right in the middle of the action. We never have to walk very far, which is good because I need to save up my energy.

It's busy everywhere, but we've been eating at all the best spots because my wife makes reservations for us. We don't have to wait in line like everybody else. Last night we had dinner at the Italian place, and we asked the server to take our photo when she brought our meals. The first shot wasn't great because my wife was getting hangry and had already started chewing, so we asked the girl to take another one. The second shot is better, although my wife's smile looks strained because she wouldn't show her teeth in case there was food in them, and for some reason the server used the flash so we're all overexposed and vampire-white. Still, she captured a moment. And the mountains and trees in the background are pristine and breathtaking.

I'd seen pictures of the Village before and thought it looked nice, but until I actually got here, I had no idea how the quaintness and charm would affect me. It feels exactly as if they've recreated an old Swiss town. Or somewhere in Norway maybe. Or France, which would make the most sense because Mont Tremblant is in the French part of Canada. Thankfully everyone speaks English here. In any case, it's stunning. We've basically stepped right into a fairy tale.

I imagine it would be even prettier in the winter. Except I don't ski. My wife does, but she's not too serious about it and it's not something we've embraced as a family. She tried taking the boys once but they hated it. Too cold, they said. They didn't like the wind in their faces.

They love it here, though. Their favourite thing is the BeaverTails. I can't even tell you how many they've eaten by now, which is sort of sickening, but hey we're here to have fun. They also tried the potato doughnuts and the gondola and they liked both of those things at first, but then the little guy puked over the side on their third trip up. My wife said it was because I told him about the potatoes in the doughnuts. I said, "Well it's an ingredient. It says so right on the sign." She said, "But he doesn't pay attention to things like that."

Which makes me think of the part of your article where you said we need to pay more attention to exactly who participates in triathlons and who doesn't. And there was that photo of a bunch of racers in a lake or an ocean somewhere—who knows the location because I didn't see a caption. I might've just been too angry to notice it. Who knows when it was taken. Even if it was recent, it was just one particular section of one particular race. And they were all in swim caps and goggles and wetsuits, so obviously they would look alike, whether they were white guys or green guys or purple guys. Yet you included it like it proved your point that only one percent of triathletes are Black.

Meanwhile, I've already seen at least four or five Black people since we arrived! Most of them were in great shape, but some of the men might've been security guards, I'm not sure. I've also seen a ton of Asians here, and you didn't even bother mentioning them. It's hard to tell who's competing unless they're wearing the backpack or have the tattoo. I guess we'll find out tomorrow morning when we all line up together on the beach, united in spite of our vast differences in age and life experiences. We'll see how hollow your empty words ring then, and how accurate your numbers are.

My wife has been in a pretty consistent good mood here, and thankfully that makes life easier for everyone. Seriously, though, I love her so much. She's quite a small woman but she's my biggest cheerleader. What I like to do when I train is, I picture her waiting for me at the finish line, and all I can hear is her high-pitched voice shouting, "You'll always be my Ironman, baby!" Which means I'm indestructible and your stupid words can't penetrate me anymore.

Do you even have any inkling about how hard I've trained for this? Or about how many vacation days I've had to use up to do that training, to the point where my partners at the firm are getting pretty pissed at me even though they've been really supportive overall—unlike yourself—of what I'm trying to accomplish? No. You have no inkling.

Also Tyler, who coaches triathletes *professionally*, believes in me one hundred percent. And yeah okay I'm paying him, but would he bullshit me if he didn't think I had a shot? I don't think so. This one time after a session, I invited Tyler in for a kombucha and he said sure. So we drank the kombucha and my wife was there with these protein powerballs she just made, and she offered one to Tyler and he said sure. He took a bite and made a face and spat it right back out and said to her, "This is fucking gross."

The man says what he means and means what he says.

He apologized after that, and he even offered to clean up

the floor, but my wife was already down there with a roll of paper towels. She told him she was trying a new recipe and she still needed to work out the kinks, so he shouldn't worry about it. And Tyler said, "I'm not."

I haven't shown my wife your article and I don't plan to. What did you even hope to gain from it? Do you think it makes you better than the rest of us? It doesn't. It makes you worse. You claim to be a fellow triathlete who loves triathlons, but your so-called "disquieting analysis of an exclusive recreational pursuit" tells me otherwise. The first time I read it, I thought to myself, *Why is this clown smiling in his author photo? He doesn't look very disquieted to me.* And any tri who truly loves this sport would definitely never call it "recreational." It's an all-consuming, serious passion for pushing the human body to its very limits.

I also thought you sort of looked like my cousin Cody, but the similarity ends there. Because Cody is a lifeguard who literally saves lives for his job and you are the opposite of that. Cody is one of the best guys I know and you are one of the worst.

You also conveniently left out the fact that Ironman gives employment to a ton of diverse people. Like our server at the Italian place, who was excellent. I asked her where she was from when she was taking our orders, but I don't think she heard me. The restaurant was pretty loud. Or maybe she wasn't from anywhere and she just had a really impressive tan.

You go on and on about privilege, but do you even understand what it means to have the privilege of losing someone special and then training hard every single day as a tribute to their memory? Last night we watched a video montage of all the participants here who are competing to honour their loved ones who've died or who are close to death due to cancer or other terrible diseases. But instead of focusing on their poignant anecdotes, all I could think about was you squatting over their loved ones' graves and hospital beds and taking a giant disrespectful shit on their pain.

Have you ever heard of something called mental health? Are you aware that it's a very serious issue, and exercise can cure it? Andy sent me an inspiring article once about a cosmetic surgeon in Italy who was extremely stressed out and overworked until he started training for Kona and then his mood totally improved. It was basically a miracle. But I guess an analytical person like you doesn't believe in miracles.

I bet you would if you were here, though. This place is magical and if anybody disagrees with that I will kick them in the face. The magic is undeniable. You've got more than a thousand exceptional examples of humanity heroically defying the boundaries of mortality, witnessed and applauded by their cherished friends and family and surrounded and embraced by Mother Nature at her most attractive. We saw a fucking DEER last night. It appeared for us out of the bush when we were out for a walk and then it disappeared again before anyone else saw it. We weren't even sure at first if it was real. My wife said, "Is that a cardboard cut-out of a deer over there?" Because that's all we'd ever seen in the city. My oldest son said, "No, Mom, it's alive!" But she wasn't convinced so he threw a few pebbles just to make it run, and when it did, the sheer wonder of that moment hit us like a sledgehammer.

Do you have any idea how deeply your words have wormed their way into my brain, making it impossible for me to be in the zone and the flow exactly when I'm supposed to be in the zone and the flow? But fuck you, and I don't even care because Tyler and I have created a system together. We've been working on it so hard for so long. Perfecting it. It's a great system, and by Christ it's going to help me win.

Oh, and by the way, Tyler's wife is Black. Just think about that for a minute. Or maybe she's just his girlfriend, I'm not sure. I've never met her. One day I'd like to invite her and Tyler over for dinner, and my wife will make pot roast and her cheesy cauliflower keto bombs. I am really looking forward to that.

Now the forecast is looking shitty for the race tomorrow. It's like you're using that technique where the mood of the writing is the same as the mood of the weather. I don't remember what it's called, but I remember learning way back in my high school English class that it was a bad technique and we should never use it.

You are not a good writer. Your words have no power over me. I wish Andy had never sent me your article, but it's too late for that now, and I don't want to use up any of my wishes on anything to do with you. So here's what I'm going to wish for: To spend this afternoon on a chaise lounge by the hotel pool and soak up the sun while my kids play with the other triathletes' kids. To enjoy a sumptuous dinner at Le Shak tonight—which I know for sure will come true because we have a reservation—followed by BeaverTails for dessert and then sex with my wife after the boys fall asleep.

And tomorrow morning, rain or shine, I'm going to wake up early feeling rested and energized. I've instructed my family to write my name on the road with sidewalk chalk along with the motivational phrases of their choice. I'm going to put on my wetsuit and take my place among the other elite athletes who have paid the entrance fee in cash and buckets of our blood, sweat, and tears.

And then my fellow competitors and I will wade into the lake together, not holding hands but technically close enough to hold hands because it will be excessively crowded. We will look nothing like the seething, splashing mass of faceless white men in your photo, elbowing each other in the faces and ribs and churning the lake into foam in their desperate flailing to get ahead of each other and secure a few precious inches of space for God's sake so they could start swimming.

Instead, we will cut through the cold water like seals. We will move gracefully and with purpose, each of our strokes precise and formidable, for exactly 3.9 kilometres, until we reach the shore on the other side and emerge to cast off our wetsuits like selkies shedding their skins. We will wave to the adoring hordes, and their roars of approval will follow us to the parking lot where our bikes are locked up. Then we'll become some other mythological being, centaurs maybe, because that's what triathletes are. We have stepped right out of a fairy tale, strong and brave and extraordinary. Taking part in something beautiful, just because we can.

SOMETHING FUN TO DO ON
A BEAUTIFUL DAY

THERE IS A BIRD IN THE WATER. Directly in front of them, on the other side of the protective barrier. The mother and the father didn't see it at first but then their little girl jumped up and down and shouted, "Look!"

The sleek dark head bobs just above the surface of the churning white-and-green rapids. Its beak is long and sharp and its eyes are black beads.

The three of them are holding on to different parts of the wide, slanted silver bars that separate them from the river and from the bird, which is farther away from them now, closer to the falls.

"It shouldn't be there," says the mother. "Should it?"

Because this part of the river is clearly not a safe place, and the bird is all alone.

"Maybe it knows what it's doing," says the father.

"What kind of a bird is it?" asks the girl, who is six years old and knows a lot of things already. She knows that if she squeezes her body between the silver bars and takes a few steps across the grass and holds her breath and jumps into the water, she will be swept away from her parents and over the waterfall and onto the rocks at the bottom and she will die.

"I don't know," says the father. "Maybe a duck?"

"It doesn't look like a duck," says the mother. "The beak is too pointy."

"It looks like it would peck me," says the daughter. "It would peck me and make a hole in my skin and then it would suck out all of my blood."

"Yikes," says the father.

"I told you she was too young for that wax museum," the mother tells him. "That stuff is in her head forever now."

The bird goes under then, and they all lean forward.

Before the falls, they'd walked through a haunted house full of wax figures posed in gruesome scenes of torture. Kids under ten got in free and the father had been excited about the deal.

"Those people weren't real. You know that, don't you?" The father bends down so his mouth is next to his daughter's ear. Otherwise he'd have to yell because the falls are suddenly very loud. Their constant, urgent rumble drowns out everything else. "None of it was real."

The girl nods but she isn't listening. She jabs a finger at the river. "There!"

The bird has resurfaced farther upstream, facing away from the falls with its beak tilted up at the bright blue sky.

It must be so tired, the mother thinks. She closes her eyes and the mist is cool on her face. The day has been so hot and the backpack with all the things their child might need is too heavy, even after she took out a few of the less important items and left them in the car. Her back is slick with sweat and her T-shirt is soaked, which everyone would see if she removed the backpack, so she doesn't. The father keeps offering to carry it for her and she keeps saying no.

They woke up this morning and decided to come here, because the weather was nice and it's the weekend and their daughter is on summer vacation, so why not go to Niagara Falls. They're going to have dinner at a restaurant later and it's a relief to not have to think up something to cook. It was a relief to just stand here, admiring the power and majesty of the waterfall. Until they saw the bird.

The father asks if there's any water in the backpack and the mother says yes, of course, that's one of the reasons it's so heavy.

"I offered to carry it," he says.

She says he can get the water himself, so he unzips the backpack and reaches in and pulls out the bottle, which is warm now because it's just a regular bottle and not one of those special thermal bottles the father keeps wanting to buy but the mother says are too expensive. The father knows it would be a bad idea to mention this, even just conversationally. Even if all he says is, *Isn't it interesting how our water got so warm so fast, even hidden away from the sun?* That would still be a bad idea.

He unscrews the cap and takes a few sips. Then he replaces the cap and makes sure it's on tight and tucks the bottle back into the bag.

The mother can sense by the redistribution of weight that he shoved it into a different spot than it was in originally, but she decides not to say anything because then the father might sigh and roll his eyes. She hates it when he does that.

"Where is it?" says the daughter. "I don't see it."

She swivels her head, and the fair skin of her neck flashes under her messy blond hair. Her hair always gets tangled in the back. The fine strands get knotted when she sleeps, but the mother has stopped trying to comb them out because when she does, their daughter screams and says it hurts. They just have to be more diligent with the conditioner, that's all.

The tourists crowding in on either side of the mother and father and daughter exclaim over the waterfall and gape in awe and smile and take lots of pictures. Nobody else is looking for the bird.

The three of them are silent, scanning for it, until the father points at a log jutting out on their side of the river. "There."

The bird has found its way to a small pool of calmer water between the log and the grassy bank. It swims in slow, lazy circles.

"Maybe it'll be able to climb out now," says the mother.

They wait to see if it will do that, but it stays where it is.

One of the scenes in the wax museum showed an emaciated man lying on his back with a chicken-wire box attached to his shaved head. There were animatronic rats inside the box and they were gnawing on his sallow face, which was spattered with fake blood and frozen in a very convincing expression of terror and pain.

"Why are those rats eating that boy?" asked the daughter.

"It's not a boy," the father said quickly. "It's a man."

"Oh."

The mother gently touched the daughter's small shoulder but the girl didn't turn around. Her hands were pressed against the viewing window and her breath was fogging up the plexiglass.

The bird disappears again and then reappears on the dangerous side of the log.

"What kind of a bird is it?" the daughter asks the father again.

He shakes his head. "I don't know."

"You could look it up on your phone," she tells him.

"You're right," he says, but his hand doesn't move toward his pocket.

Once, about a year ago, the daughter asked him, *Do you love me, Daddy?* And he said, as a joke, *I don't know. Let me check my phone.* He made a big show of taking the device out of his pocket and tapping away on it and staring at the screen, until she started to cry.

The bird is running out of energy. It struggles against the current for only a short time before it goes limp and allows itself to be carried closer to the falls.

"It's almost at the end now," says the daughter, and her voice is so sad.

The mother doesn't like museums because of the time last year when their daughter got lost. There was a long tunnel that snaked into a kid-sized model of an Egyptian pyramid, and the father was sure there was only one way in and one way out so he wasn't worried about it, but the mother wasn't so sure. Their daughter crawled into the tunnel and disappeared, and the two of them stood by its dark mouth and waited.

After a few minutes the mother said, "Maybe there's a different exit on the other side. One of us should go and check."

"She's fine," said the father. "Let her explore."

"I'm glad she's exploring," said the mother. "I just don't want her to get lost."

"This is a museum for children," he said. "Don't you think they'd design it with that kind of thing in mind?"

"I would certainly hope so," she said. "But I don't know."

Out in the middle of the seething river, the bird's long neck strains. Its invisible feet kick uselessly beneath the rushing water. Every so often, a few stray leaves or a broken branch will swirl around it and then speed away, careening over the edge and vanishing into the mist.

When their daughter still hadn't emerged from the pyramid, the father sprinted as fast as he could to the security booth. He had trouble asking for help at first because he was out of breath. The mother was sobbing by then, and he kept telling her everything would be all right, but when their daughter finally reappeared and hurtled toward them, all the strength went out of his legs and he fell to his knees and wept before he could stop himself.

The sun beats down and the mother asks the father to take the sunscreen out of the backpack because it's time to reapply. The sky is so blue and their daughter's shoulders are too pink and there's no shade anywhere. There aren't any trees nearby and there isn't even a single cloud.

The father pulls out the can and feels briefly unsettled by the logo, a cartoon pair of sunglasses with eyes. Then he presses the nozzle and focuses the spray on their daughter's exposed skin.

When he's done, the bird goes under again. It stays underwater for a longer stretch this time, and the three of them hold their breath until it resurfaces.

Earlier in the day, soon after they arrived and found free parking at the casino, they'd bought ice cream from a man who told them that his own young daughter got very sick and then died on the boat ride over here from their home country.

"I'm so sorry," said the mother.

"Thank you for the ice cream," said the father.

The man nodded and rubbed his black beard with both of his large hands, and the mother felt bad for wanting him to sanitize before he scooped their cones.

Their little girl was playing a few metres away from the man's cart, which was decorated with colourful pictures of frozen treats. She was hopping on one foot and then the other, and the sun lit up her hair.

The man's voice was soft and mournful, and he counted out their change very carefully before he gave it to them.

They didn't ask him what country because that felt like a rude question.

The bird is so far away from them now, just a tiny dark speck on the frothing river. They can't see its beak or its eyes anymore. They can't tell what direction it's facing.

After they'd finished their ice cream, the daughter's hands were sticky, so the mother went to ask the man for some extra napkins, but she stopped. Because when she looked over, he was laughing with someone, after he had told them that his child had died.

So she wondered if that story was true. But why would he lie to them? He didn't want anything from them. He didn't even have a tip jar.

But there he was, laughing with his friend. Maybe they were telling jokes in another language. They were so happy, whereas the mother was so miserable and hot and angry that she always had to be the one to remember to pack things like wet wipes, but she hadn't packed any today so now she'd have to dump some water from one of their almost-empty bottles onto their daughter's sticky hands. But they could just buy more water somewhere. The water they brought was getting too warm to drink, anyway.

The waterfall roars, and the daughter peers between the silver bars and speaks to the faraway bird in a quiet voice so nobody else can hear. She tells it to be brave, to spread its wings and fly if it can.

She says a long time ago she was very scared too, when she could hear her parents' voices but they couldn't hear hers. She was shouting for them, but lots of other kids were shouting too so it didn't matter. She tried to calm herself down and admire the inside of the pyramid, which was really interesting. The room was small and cool and its walls were slanted. In the middle of the floor was a long box with a face on it, which was where the mummy lived. She had to crouch down to fit through the tiny door that looked like the way out, and when she stood up and blinked in the bright light on the other side, she was all alone.

But the bird doesn't fly. It doesn't do anything. The fast-moving water sweeps it away and there it goes, and now it's right at the edge and then it's gone.

"What's going to happen?" the girl asks her mother and father, even though she knows the answer.

It wouldn't matter what they said, anyway, because the boom of the waterfall is all she can hear. It's the only noise and it's everywhere.

THE MEETING

I DON'T BELIEVE IN DISCRIMINATION. If you're a person, you're a person. That's just the way I feel.

I don't care about people's differences. It doesn't bother me. I only care about what makes us all the same. We all want love, for instance. That's a big one. We all want to provide a good life for our families. We all want our children to be happy and successful.

And we all have to work hard to achieve that. Nobody said life was easy. I don't like my job, but I'm stuck there now and I don't complain. Well, I try not to. Wine helps. Haha.

Graham says nobody should get a free pass and I agree with him. Nobody should get a leg up over anybody else because that's not fair. Graham says, "If everyone has an equal shot, then we all have an equal playing field." Which doesn't quite make sense. But you get the gist.

There is also luck, of course. Luck visits different people in different ways.

For instance, I could've ended up married to Tommy, but he was run over by a car. And thank God for that because our relationship was extremely unhealthy and I definitely didn't realize it at the time. I would've followed Tommy to the ends of the Earth and back again if he'd asked me to, and he wouldn't have asked nicely and I wouldn't even have cared. Because I was wild about him, and Graham is fine, but we just don't have the same spark that I had with Tommy. Where is the fire? Anyway, you make your peace with things.

There is a mom who I always see at the daycare at pickup time, and one day I'm going to introduce myself and ask her the secret to her marriage. Because she and her husband are always laughing together and she is always touching his arm, which is something I've never thought to do with Graham. I don't even notice his arms. They just hang there.

Except no, sometimes I notice how light Graham's arm hair is compared with how dark Tommy's arm hair was. Dark and thick. Tommy was Italian.

I find my husband attractive, don't get me wrong. We both have Nordic roots and everybody jokes we could be IKEA catalogue models, isn't that funny? But most days I'm just happier on my own. He goes to his job and I go to my job, and he's with the people he's with every day and I'm with the people I'm with every day. I like my co-workers well enough, and most of us see eye-to-eye on things so we have pleasant conversations in snippets and we send each other silly emails. Then I leave and I pick up the kids and I meet Graham at home and we all have dinner. Usually takeout because I'm worn out by that point. We take turns putting the kids to bed and then we watch TV and then it's time to go to sleep. Sometimes we have sex and it's often reasonably satisfying.

But this couple has something special. They moved here from Scarborough with their son a few months ago, is what I've heard, and apparently they're both scientists, which is exciting. They're always together so that's why I haven't introduced myself to the mom yet, but one day I will. She seems nice and she's so pretty. I keep meaning to say hello and tell her she looks like Rihanna. Because she does! They could be twins.

What she has with her husband (who looks like a young Denzel Washington in that movie where he was a rogue detective, what was it called? I loved that movie, it was so action-packed!) reminds me of what I used to have with Tommy, minus the bad stuff, and sometimes that makes me feel regretful even though I know he was not a good man and it's for the best that he died. He used to call me awful names and I didn't speak up for myself. I would just smile and take it.

We used to go out dancing and drink way too much cheap draft, and once Tommy got so drunk that he accidentally burned my hand with his cigarette while we were making out to a Killers song. I still have the scar and sometimes I'll rub it and think about that night. He got into a fight later outside the bar and the police had to come and break it up. The blood on both men was all lit up red and blue and the cops were shouting, "Go home and sleep it off, boys!" Then when we got back to Tommy's grubby apartment he pushed me down on the filthy floor and attacked me like a rabid dog. The sex was always exhilarating. I never knew what he was going to do to me. That part of it was good. Everything else was bad.

But then I met Graham and now we have two beautiful children together! And they're good kids, mostly. They're not mean to anybody, except that one time during Beavers when Wyatt did that thing to that other boy, but the Beaver leader didn't let that slide. He made Wyatt apologize and then he told him, in no uncertain terms, that what he had done was unacceptable. The Beaver leader communicated this to me and Graham in an email after the fact. So by then it felt too late to reprimand Wyatt ourselves. When they're that young, if the timing of your anger doesn't match up with the timing of their misbehaviour, that can be very confusing and upsetting for them.

Scarlett hits her brother sometimes, but we're not concerned about that. If it was Wyatt hitting Scarlett, then we would be more concerned. Though by this point he'd be well within his rights to smack her back and call it self-defence. Graham and I keep waiting to see if he'll do it. But so far we've been disappointed.

There are always two sides to every story. So when I heard about the incident at the school, I was disturbed, certainly. But I wanted to reserve judgment until I had all the details.

I still don't have all the details, so all I can do is guess.

A teacher said something to a student, apparently, but I'm not sure what because I didn't go to the meeting. There was a meeting last week about the incident but I was busy scrapbooking that night so I couldn't go. But my friend Trish was going so I asked her to tell me about it later. But then she couldn't because everyone at the meeting agreed not to talk about it with anybody else because of privacy. Trish was only able to tell me that prejudice was involved. Which of course was quite shocking.

"Who was prejudiced against who?" I asked her when we met up for coffee and Danishes on the weekend.

She shook her head slowly from side to side. "We're not allowed to say."

"Hmm." I stirred my vanilla-bean frappuccino harder than I needed to. "Were there consequences?"

"It's not my place to share that information." She took a sip of her flat white and I swear she gave me a smug little mi-crofoamy smile but I couldn't be one hundred per cent sure.

I looked out the window. Lots of families were walking their dogs. Scarlett and Wyatt really want a dog but I hate dogs so we will never get one.

Lately I've been researching guinea pigs because maybe a guinea pig will bring joy to my family. By all accounts they have a sweet and loving nature and like to be cuddled. And when you get tired of them, you can just put them back in their cage. And when they die, the kids will learn about death. I'm not so keen on the idea of handling a dead guinea pig because I worry it might feel like a bean bag with spiky feet. But I could wear gloves. A guinea pig would be more work than a hamster, but hamsters are nocturnal and we're pretty strict with Scarlett and Wyatt's bedtime schedule. If we had to keep them up later just to play with a hamster because that's the best time for the hamster, then what would that teach them? I'm not sure. There might be some lesson there, something about love or respect or patience or all those things combined, but Scarlett and Wyatt really need their sleep. And I need them to go to sleep by a certain time so I can do what I want to do, which is watch something stupid on Netflix and not feel beholden to anyone for an hour before I go to bed myself. Graham and I watch our own shows in separate rooms at night and sometimes I think maybe that hour would be a nice time to have together, just the two of us, but maybe not. Maybe we wouldn't enjoy that time and then we'd just feel worse.

"I can tell you one thing." Trish leaned toward me across our small circular table, and the movement was so sudden and forceful that our plates clinked against each other. "The mom was really angry."

I felt my eyes widen. It was a strange cartoon feeling. "What was she angry about?"

"Sorry." She poked a finger into her Danish and scooped out some of the cherry filling. "Can't tell you." Then she opened her mouth and licked her finger clean.

My mind reeled with the possibilities.

Then we got gabbing about work and our husbands and our kids and how we never have enough time for ourselves, and we started planning a long-overdue girls' weekend at Trish's cottage and we got super excited about that so we stopped talking about the incident even though I was still thinking about it.

I am pretty sure it involved the son of the mom I always see at the daycare at pickup time.

It's just a hunch. There's no way to confirm it. But that's what I think. Her son goes to Wyatt and Scarlett's school. I could ask Scarlett and Wyatt about it but he's not in either of their classes, and anyway neither of them is very observant.

I could ask the mom. But she's always with her husband so I haven't introduced myself to her yet. But I want to. And then I could ask her.

I'm full of questions lately.

At our most recent parent-council meeting, we were trying to brainstorm ways to make the school feel more inclusive after the principal suggested that was something we should think about. But then we got distracted when Trish's friend Beatrice started crying. We asked her what was wrong and she told us that her property had been vandalized the night before.

We live in a very safe area, so this was big news.

Beatrice discovered the damage when she left the house that morning to walk her kids to school. Her youngest daughter screamed and pointed at the old-fashioned jockey statue on their front lawn because the head had been spray-painted white and then a "scary face" had been drawn on with red ink.

There was a collective intake of breath around the table, and a few seconds of stunned silence as we all struggled to process this. We widened our eyes and covered our mouths with our hands.

"That's horrific," said Trish.

"Poor Oaklee," I said. "She must've been traumatized."

"She was." Beatrice nodded, her voice trembling. "We all were."

"Just dreadful," said Helen, who is Greek. We love her because she always brings honey balls to the meetings, but nobody wanted to eat any right at that moment.

Beatrice jiggled her head back and forth and up and down, as if she were trying to shake the image of the ruined jockey out of her mind. "Why would anyone *do* that?"

We patted her on the arm and murmured various words of comfort, and Denise who lives up the street from me said we should all get doorbell cameras installed, which is something

Graham has already been talking about but we have an alarm system so I didn't see the need for it but now I definitely do, but none of us had an answer for Beatrice's question.

Then Rowena put her hand up, which was a dumb thing to do because we're all adults, but that's Rowena for you. Rowena with her hippie clothes and her hippie scarves that she ties into her frizzy hair all the time like she was a child of the sixties, except she's younger than we are. Not much younger, though.

Trish sighed. "Yes, Rowena?"

None of us really likes Rowena because she's the secretary and when she takes the minutes her face is always overly expressive, like she's passing judgment on the things we're saying. Trish and Beatrice are the co-chairs and I'm the treasurer and we take our roles very seriously. We wish Rowena would do the same.

"I think," said Rowena, who doesn't usually say very much, "I think...some people might find those types of statues offensive?"

"That's ridiculous," said Trish.

"Exactly." Beatrice sniffled. "He was just a cute little man who welcomed us home with his cute little lantern. But now he's a monster." She glared at Rowena. "And it was an antique. It was my mother's, and my mother is dead."

Rowena didn't reply and we were glad. She kept her head down and quietly took her notes with her tie-dyed scarf flopping over her eyes.

We wrapped things up after that. There were still a bunch of items on our agenda, but Beatrice was distraught by then and it just didn't feel right for us to tackle anything else.

The main thing is that we're all good neighbours here, and we have a very supportive school community too. And if certain people don't feel like joining the parent council for whatever reason, then that's their call and that's their business. It's not because we're not welcoming. It's a big commitment and we're all volunteers and we work hard to organize the fall barbecue and the spring fun fair and the student art auction and the movie nights in between. We even have a popcorn machine. And it's nobody's fault if somebody complains anonymously to the principal that the movies aren't diverse enough, because we are trying to appeal to the majority. That's the only fair thing in this situation. We all have lives and families and full-time or part-time jobs, so we can only do what we can do. We are good people who care deeply about our children's education and we have great affection and respect for the teachers and the school staff and our fellow parents and caregivers, no matter what.

And there she is! She just arrived. That mom.

But where's her husband? It's odd that he's not here. Mysterious, even.

I have never seen them not together. Graham came with me to daycare pickup exactly once, two years ago, when we were on our way to the airport to take the kids on the Disney cruise.

Is she wearing heels? She looks taller today. And her hair is different again. Sometimes it's long and sometimes it's short and I'm so confused about how that can be possible.

I think she might've noticed me looking at her so now I'm looking at my phone. Was I staring? I'm sure I wasn't staring. I was just looking. I could've been looking at anyone.

There is nothing interesting on my phone. Graham texted me the peach emoji earlier today but I haven't responded.

I'll introduce myself to her another day. The kids are starting to come out now, anyway.

Why is daycare pickup always my responsibility? Graham's schedule is flexible.

There's her son. He's always smiling. He runs straight over to his mom and they embrace like they've been apart for years.

Meanwhile I'm still waiting for my own children. Scarlett and Wyatt are always the last ones out because they're always fighting so it takes them forever to pack up and get their coats on. I told the staff to separate them but my kids aren't good listeners.

The boy finally stops hugging his mom, and then he looks around with a furrowed brow. He's probably wondering where his dad is. I'm wondering too. He's always here. Why isn't he here today?

Aha! *Training Day*! That was the Denzel Washington movie. So violent! I knew I'd remember—it was right on the tip of my tongue.

Now the mom is bending down and whispering in her son's ear and I wish I knew what she was saying because now he's laughing, and the sound is loud and joyous and bounces across the parking lot and for a long moment it's all I can hear.

But then I hear something else. A high-pitched yip-yip-yipping noise that hurts my ears, and I turn in the direction of where it's coming from, and there is the dad. He was there all along, waiting in the car. He's walking over now, and he's holding a puppy.

The boy lets out a whoop of delight and runs toward him, and the mom and dad are grinning at each other, and soon the family is surrounded by daycare kids and their parents all oohing and aahing over the adorable tiny fluffball.

And here come my kids, yelling at me to take their backpacks. Any minute now they're going to spot the puppy and they'll stroke its super-soft fur and then tonight I'll have to listen to them whining at me again to get a dog.

Maybe we'll get one, I don't know. But they'll have to take care of it because I won't.

I'm frowning at the family now and I don't even care if they see me.

They're not paying attention, anyway.

Scarlett cried non-stop during that Disney cruise, it was horrible. Wyatt would only eat Froot Loops, which they only served at breakfast. We had to squirrel away bowls and bowls of Froot Loops for him to eat at lunch and dinner, and then his poop turned blue and Scarlett got scared and started wailing when she saw it in the toilet when we forgot to flush one time.

In retrospect, neither of them was old enough to enjoy any of it.

SWIMMING LESSON

THE TANTRUM BEGINS IN THE MALL, where so many tantrums begin. The mall is where the worst tantrums are basically guaranteed. Sometimes Stacey even gets two! BOGO half-price tantrums.

Her daughter Adelaide, provider of the tantrum, is five. Old enough to put her parents into hysterics when she gives her French fries hilariously elaborate names like Lady Bertha Pickle Pie and Glory Rose Suitcase Head and engages them in long, emotional conversations with each other before biting down and making them scream. But still young enough to go into hysterics herself when she doesn't get her way.

It's because she doesn't want to go to her swimming lesson. That's why Adelaide started whining inside the mall and why she escalated to shrieking as soon as they got outside.

Now she is kicking the back of the driver's seat while Stacey tries to focus on the road and navigate through traffic that is far busier and more ruthless than she had expected. A red sedan cuts her off and she blasts the horn and says, as calmly as possible, "Please don't do that. I don't like that."

Her furious daughter has not yet offered a reason for her opposition to the swimming lesson. She will only yell, "I don't want to go to swimming!" over and over again.

Stacey is trying to get an explanation.

Because normally, under every other circumstance, Adelaide loves swimming. It's one of her favourite things to do and she's good at it. Not good enough yet to stay alive in a body of water, but pretty damn good for a five-year-old.

So why doesn't she want to go to the swimming lesson? Because she's still angry at her mother for not buying her that freakishly hideous headband from The Children's Place? The one with the leopard-print tulle flower scrunched onto it? *My God*, Stacey thinks, *that thing was ugly*. Her daughter has a different fashion sense than she does, though. Arguably a much better one. But still. That headband.

∽

The girl at the cash only made things worse by telling Adelaide how cute she looked with it on, "like a tiny Taylor Swift!" and Adelaide beamed even though she has no idea who Taylor Swift is. Stacey knows she's a singer but that's about it.

She'd smiled at the pretty young woman with her piercings and her complicated pile of blond hair framing her zombie-pale face and said, "Thank you, but we're just here to buy some tops and underwear."

The girl winked at Adelaide like they were best friends and then rang up the tops and underwear. Adelaide was still wearing the headband, and Stacey told her to take it off.

"No," said Adelaide.

"Was anyone helping you with this today?"

"Oh." Stacey blinked at the cashier and glanced over at the two other pretty young women folding T-shirts together. "Yes. She was."

"Which one?"

"Um."

"The Black girl or the white girl?"

"Mama," said Adelaide. "Please!"

"No," said Stacey, then mumbled, "Black girl," very quietly as she removed the headband and took her bag and grabbed her daughter's hand and hauled her out of the store.

∽

This is Adelaide's first time taking swimming lessons with no parents in the pool—just the students and the instructor —and this is the third lesson of the term.

Stacey and Christopher went together to the first class and cheered and clapped from the wooden bleachers as Adelaide did everything she was supposed to, and the whole time she seemed to be lit up with barely controllable glee.

Stacey had thought to herself, perched next to her husband as he made goofy faces at their daughter, *I don't like that the instructor has to touch her all the time.*

The instructor is a young guy, maybe in his early twenties. He smiles constantly. And he wasn't touching the students in a suspicious way. Just in a normal, I-will-teach-you-how-to-swim way. Because he has to. And he seems great. Sweet with the kids—all three of them are girls— and very encouraging.

Christopher took Adelaide to the second lesson by himself because Stacey had to work, and Christopher said, "It's okay, it's fine! You stay home and do your work and we'll go by ourselves and we'll miss you a lot but don't worry, we'll survive." So she wasn't there to observe that one.

The traffic slows, and Stacey presses the brake and reaches for her phone.

She texts Christopher, even though she knows she should not be texting in the car. Texting while driving is idiotic and dangerous. But she texts him now, *Hi! She had fun at swimming last week, right?*

He texts right back, *Hey there! Yep, she had a blast!* He uses that word, *blast*, and puts an exclamation mark after it.

She shouldn't be surprised either, because he told her all about it last week. He was bursting to tell her about how much fun Adelaide had, and how she did a bob for the first time ever and she didn't even complain about getting her hair wet. And they smiled at each other and murmured about her amazingness.

His enthusiastic reply is reassuring. Everything must be fine with the swimming lessons, then.

She puts her phone face down on the passenger seat and focuses on the line of cars in front of her and behind her and asks her daughter again, "Why don't you want to go to swimming?"

"Because I don't want to!" Another outraged kick to the back of her seat, more vicious this time.

Stacey swerves to avoid a silver minivan trying to merge into her lane. She thinks of the rainbow-striped metal water bottle in Adelaide's cup holder and wonders if Adelaide might throw it at her and cause an accident. No, she wouldn't do that. She has never done anything like that.

But the potential for this violence shimmers between them, and Stacey feels her daughter's rage entering her bloodstream, the heat of it spreading everywhere and making her grind her teeth.

She needs to say something now.

So she proceeds to tell her daughter in a low, serious voice that she needs to learn to be more grateful for everything she has. Because some children have nothing. They don't even get food.

"No *food*?" says Adelaide.

And Stacey thrills that she is getting through to her, that her wisdom is being digested.

Then Adelaide snarls and kicks the driver's seat again and Stacey pounds the steering wheel and shouts, "That's it!"

She is hot all over and she flicks on the air conditioning as the words boil up and out, her jaw stiff with fury and barely moving as she enunciates to her daughter that she *will* go to her swimming lesson, and if she misbehaves when she is there, her mother will *not* take her to the restaurant after for a treat. Instead they will go straight home and the child will go straight to bed with no dinner and no stories. Period.

"No I won't!" Adelaide screeches.

"Yes, you will."

"It's too cold in here!"

Shut up, Stacey wants to say, but she doesn't. She has never said anything like that.

Adelaide starts to cry.

Sweat prickles across Stacey's hairline. She tilts the vent and cranks the fan up all the way.

It's chilly outside but it's not winter yet.

Two months ago, Adelaide started senior kindergarten. Just breezed right in this time, like it was nothing. For the entire first half of junior kindergarten, she wailed every single morning and Stacey had to rush over and give her one last hug before saying goodbye.

Stacey angles the rear-view mirror so she can see her daughter, who is slumped in her car seat, staring out the window with tears on her round, rosy cheeks.

"Because you don't make the big decisions," Stacey says, mostly to herself. "Mommy and Daddy make the big decisions. Not you."

They sit in silence for a while and the traffic keeps crawling, and Stacey thinks how sad it is that nobody wiggles their fingers in the rear-view mirror anymore at their fellow drivers who let them in. She still does it, but the windows are tinted so they probably can't see her, anyway.

There are a few pitiful sniffles from the back seat, and she listens for what will come next.

"Mama?"

"Yes?"

"How about no swimming and no restaurant. Just home." Then an achingly hopeful pause. "Deal?"

Stacey switches off the air conditioning. The fury ebbs away and leaves her limp and disoriented, like it always does. "Please tell me why you don't want to go to swimming."

"Because I don't want to!"

Stacey takes a deep breath. "Do you like your teacher?"

No answer.

"Honey? Do you like your swimming teacher?"

"One thumb up and one thumb down."

This is not a satisfactory response. "Why is one thumb down?"

No answer.

Stacey keeps driving. Up ahead, there's an exit she could take that would turn them around and point them in the direction of their house, but she drives past it.

Because it would be silly not to go to the swimming lesson. It would mean she was giving in.

Adelaide is quiet. There is only the whoosh of cars going by—faster now—and the occasional clink of the water bottle when she picks it up for a sip and then puts it back.

Stacey hasn't told Christopher that she doesn't like that the swimming instructor touches their daughter because he would say she worries too much. He would say of course the guy has to touch her, because it's his job. And she would have to agree.

They are almost at the recreation centre. It's nearly time for Stacey to park and get out of the car and unbuckle Adelaide from her car seat and lead her into the building and down the dim hallway to the change room. There she will help Adelaide take off her clothes and put on her bathing suit, even though her daughter is perfectly capable by now of doing that herself. And then Stacey will bundle all their stuff together into a clumsy pile and carry everything out with them because there are no lockers here. And then they will walk together to the pool.

∽

Stacey is lucky because nothing bad has ever happened to her.

Well, things have happened. But not like that. Not compared to some people.

Well, some bad things. But not really. They are things she can look back on and say, "That wasn't so bad."

There was the time long ago when her dad's friend sat beside her on her parents' bed.

It was when she had a fever, and she was watching *The Dukes of Hazzard* on her parents' little black-and-white TV, and the adults were all supposed to be in the living room drinking wine.

The friend sat down very close to her, and the mattress sunk under his weight. He asked her, "How are you feeling?"

She shrugged. She kept her eyes on Luke and Bo with their jeans and cowboy hats and their plaid shirts that showed their chests. She had a crush on both brothers but mostly on Luke. She liked that his name rhymed. Luke Duke.

∽

Stacey is sitting in the stands now, and Adelaide is in the pool. The parking and unbuckling and walking and changing part has happened already and Adelaide co-operated through all of it. She seems happy and relaxed in the water with the instructor and the other kids, so Stacey relaxes a little too.

She chose this recreation centre specifically for these lessons because the parents are allowed to watch. In other locations, there's not enough room.

Other parents have told her they don't mind waiting where they can't see the pool. They can get a lot done in that half-hour. "We can all use the break, right?" they say, and Stacey has to agree.

Other parents have also started dropping off their kids at playdates and birthday parties and leaving them there. Adelaide has apparently reached that age already. The alternative is the adults having to stand around and make awkward conversation, which no one wants to do. The parents who stay, like Stacey does, are a burden.

The swimming instructor is clowning around now, telling his students to splash him. They giggle as he shuts his eyes and shakes the water off his close-cropped black hair. Then he dribbles water onto the girls' heads, one by one. He's getting them used to how it feels.

It's uncomfortable at first, Stacey imagines him saying, *but then it's okay*. She can't hear him from where she's sitting, though, so she doesn't know for sure.

She leaves Adelaide at school all day, but that's different. Because she has to. It helps that, so far, the teachers have all been women.

And Stacey knows so many good men. They are all so good. Loving and devoted and protective, and she can look at each one of them and know that they are not the problem. They are actually the opposite of the problem. Although there are really only four of them—Stacey's dad and Christopher's dad and two friends that either she or Christopher has known since childhood—that she would leave her daughter alone with, ever.

This makes her feel mean. Out of all of these good men that Stacey knows, there are only *four*?

Of course, she could probably leave Adelaide alone with seventy-five per cent of them and nothing would ever happen. Ninety per cent, even. Or eighty.

Stacey feels like an asshole when she thinks these things, but she can't help it.

It's the strangers, though, that she has no barometer for.

All she can do is sit in the stands with her nose full of chlorine and her glasses fogging up from the humidity, and she has to keep taking them off and wiping them so she can see everything. So she can scrutinize what the swimming instructor is doing and keep watch over Adelaide's small, round bum sticking up out of the water as she kicks her legs—she is learning to kick so well!—and then she shifts her gaze to the instructor's hands and where they locate themselves on her daughter, because of course he has to hold the children he's in charge of, that's ridiculous, of course he does. It's his job to teach them how to swim and to prevent them from drowning.

"Do you think he teaches adults?"

Stacey frowns at the voice, a fly buzzing in her right ear. She doesn't want to be distracted.

But the woman keeps talking. "Maybe he could give us private lessons."

Reluctantly, Stacey turns toward the source of the noise. "Pardon me?"

The woman arches a sculpted brow. Her complexion is as fair as Stacey's, but somehow it glows under the unflattering fluorescent lighting that completely washes Stacey out. The woman's cheeks are flushed but she isn't shiny with perspiration like Stacey is. She's even wearing a cable-knit cardigan and tall, pointy boots. Stacey can only wear a T-shirt here because otherwise she'd be drenched. And she always changes into flip-flops because street shoes aren't allowed.

She gives the woman the briefest smile of acknowledgement and turns her attention back to the pool.

"I can't stop staring either. Fuck me, look at him."

Stacey flinches even though her daughter is far away. She and Christopher always try not to swear around Adelaide, and mostly they're successful.

The instructor places his large palms on Adelaide's tiny waist again, to help ease her off the edge of the pool and back into the water.

She doesn't remember noticing the contrast before, but she must have. His dark-brown hands against her daughter's pale-peachy limbs. Of course she noticed.

Is that why she was worried? She wants to think the answer is no but now she isn't sure.

She had noticed that the recreation centre happens to be in a more multicultural neighbourhood than the one where she and her family live, but she certainly wasn't concerned about that at all. She's only concerned because her daughter is a girl and the instructor is a man, and that's all there is to it.

∽

Before the first swim class started, Stacey had stood on the pool deck in her flip-flops holding Adelaide's hand. Christopher sat up in the bleachers because he didn't think it was necessary to speak with the instructor before the lessons started, but Stacey did. They were a few minutes early, so Stacey and Adelaide were alone on the tiles while three attractive and athletic twentysomethings wearing *SWIM COACH* T-shirts over their swimsuits bustled around behind the window of the small staff room. The two young women were laughing together and the young man was shaking his head at them and grinning.

Please, not him, Stacey had thought, but not for the bad reason she was thinking about now.

Because the young women had brown skin too. So that part definitely didn't matter.

Then the young man walked out holding a clipboard with Adelaide's name on it and Stacey smiled at him with too much exuberance. "I just wanted to meet you," she said quickly. "This is her first lesson without a parent in the pool."

"Don't worry." The instructor had nodded solemnly. "She'll be okay."

∽

The annoying woman beside her smirks and fans herself in an exaggerated way. "It's soooo hot in here!"

Stacey slides left along the wooden bench, too quickly. She could easily get a splinter but she doesn't care. She knows she is not this woman, but she also knows there are thoughts inside her that she shouldn't have but she has them anyway.

She keeps going until the woman disappears from her peripheral vision. Until she can only see what's directly in front of her, and there's nothing to hear but splashing and squealing and hoots and hollers and gravel spraying up from the tires as the General Lee fishtailed.

∽

A chase scene was starting, which was exciting, but she looked away from the TV when her dad's friend uncrossed his legs.

His hands were worm-pink and freckled, and he lifted one and placed it on her forehead and said, "Oh dear, you're burning up." Then he reached for the remote with his other hand and turned up the volume.

The banjo music got louder and Stacey waited for him to call her mom into the room to take her temperature and give her some medicine, but he didn't.

He left his big palm on her small face, and then he slid it down her right cheek and dragged his thick fingers across her lips, which were very dry. She always remembers how dry her lips were because his skin was damp and she didn't like that. She wouldn't open her mouth for his thumb with its sharp, dirty nail, even when he pressed harder and it hurt.

And then her mom was standing in the doorway and asking her if she was feeling any better, and if the episode was a good one and did the sheriff do something stupid again this time?

And her dad's friend stood up and walked out and didn't say anything, but her mom said to him, "Sharon says it's getting late. I think she's ready to go," and the friend nodded. And her mom looked over at her, not smiling but not doing anything else either. She was just there, and then she stepped into the room and clicked the volume down, and then she left. And Stacey went back to watching the show, and yes, of course the sheriff was doing something stupid again. Of course he was, because that was what always happened.

Stacey thinks she was probably around nine years old then, since that was the age when she liked to eat a giant bowl of green olives with the pimentos removed and watch *The Dukes of Hazzard*. She didn't eat any olives that night, though, because of the fever.

Her dad's friend never came over again, not for wine or anything else.

∽

The instructor positions Adelaide's hands on the bright yellow railing of the platform that the littlest kids have to stand on so they won't go under.

Stacey doesn't think any of his touches are gratuitous. They really do appear to be just part of him doing his job. He isn't touching her daughter in any of the areas that would sound an alarm.

Besides all that, Adelaide looks completely elated. She is jumping up and down, being sweetly careful not to splash the other girls. Every few minutes she waves exuberantly at her mom, and sometimes she blows kisses too.

Stacey waves back and smiles. She can tell that her daughter is proud of herself. She can tell that she's having a blast.

The tantrum from earlier was just a tantrum. Just another power play. It's obvious now. Stacey wouldn't let Adelaide have the headband and then Adelaide got mad.

Stacey makes a show of catching her daughter's kiss as it rockets toward her.

She needs to figure out a way to teach Adelaide to be more grateful, because gratitude is everything.

The instructor blows a whistle and lifts each of the girls out of the pool. He grasps them gently under their arms and hoists them onto the smooth blue tile, and all three students scramble to their feet and grimace at their caregivers with chattering teeth.

Stacey stands up and shuffles sideways off the bench, carrying all of their stuff. She plods down the concrete steps and then the woman from before is beside her again, and Stacey reddens and swerves to avoid her gaze.

Now Adelaide is walking toward her—not running because running isn't allowed—and she's beaming and shivering, and Stacey rushes over with the hooded duck towel and kneels down and wraps her up in it.

For a moment, only her daughter's impossibly luminous face is visible from within her terry-cloth cocoon. Stacey remembers the days of swaddling and is mostly glad that those days are over. She is not one of those mothers who misses the baby stage, because there is so much more to her child now. There is the widening of her clear green eyes, and the broadening of her wild, uneven grin, and the opening of her delicate arms that Stacey likes to encircle with her thumb and forefinger and marvel at how soft they are, with their poky chicken-bone elbows.

"Come here," she says to Adelaide. "Come here, come here, you did such a good job."

They hold on to each other and Stacey is wet now too but of course that doesn't matter.

"We'll go and have French fries and a milkshake," Stacey says. "Would you like that? Let's call Daddy and tell him how well you did. Let's call him on our way to the car."

Her daughter burrows closer, pressing her cheek against her mother's. The moist air glues them together and Stacey closes her eyes.

After what feels like a long time, Adelaide's muffled voice reaches for her from far away. "Mama?"

"Yes?"

"Can I get the toy with it?"

Stacey blinks under the artificial light and says yes as she pulls away. She takes her daughter's hand and they walk back to the change room together.

The woman is in there with one of the girls from Adelaide's class. She nods at Stacey, and Stacey nods back, but only out of politeness.

She wrangles Adelaide out of her wet suit and into her dry clothes. Stacey puts her own socks and sneakers back on and drops her soggy, slimy flip-flops into a plastic bag.

"I never take my shoes off here." The woman is lounging on a bench with her long legs crossed. "What are they going to do, kick us out?"

Stacey ignores her, but then Adelaide waves at the other little girl, who is getting changed all by herself, and the other little girl waves back.

"We should exchange numbers," the woman says with a wink. "Get these kiddos together for a playdate sometime." She pulls her phone out of her jeans pocket and waits with her long red nails poised over the small, bright screen.

Stacey doesn't want to, but she opens up her purse because it's easier that way. She takes out her phone, and the woman smiles.

Stacey smiles back. Because the lesson is over for today, and everything is fine.

Everything is definitely fine.

A WARM AND LIGHTHEARTED FEELING

PEOPLE ARE TALKING ABOUT A VIRUS. There have been so many viruses for so long but nobody has cared about any of them as much as they seem to care about this one.

On her subway ride to work, Joy reads in the newspaper that some parents are angry that their kids can't wear face masks at school. The school board says this would cause a panic so let's hold off on masks for now, and the parents are angry because they want to protect their kids from the kids whose parents have family in the country where the virus came from. Of course it's not those other kids' fault, they say. But they still want to be safe and take precautions. Why won't the school board allow them to take precautions? Doesn't the school board want their children to be safe?

Joy hadn't considered this but now she does, and she starts to panic a little. Her son is in Grade 5 and her daughter is in Grade 3, and she pictures them in their classrooms surrounded by deadly germs, which of course would be invisible but in the image Joy has conjured they look like gigantic swooping bats with fangs, and her pulse quickens but she's able to calm herself down by taking deep breaths and trying to be mindful. She folds up the newspaper and looks at all the different faces around her. Not making eye contact but just looking and appreciating that they are all here together in this moment, sweating on the subway in their winter coats, and everyone is so multicultural and that's really nice.

She is on her way to her office job in a tall glass building where she sits in a cubicle in front of her computer all day surrounded by the same old faces, and this daily commute in the company of people from all walks of life is something she never takes for granted. Sometimes she smiles at one of her fellow passengers and they smile back, and she feels as if an understanding has passed between them. This makes her feel good about the world, and better about her life in general.

Joy doesn't like her office job, and being a parent is exhausting. But when she imagines that—despite their diverse backgrounds—the other commuters around her have similar concerns, her heart swells with love and hope for the future, and she stops worrying so much about climate change and this new virus everyone is talking about. Not to mention the looming school strike that means, if it happens, she will have to hire a babysitter for her two children, and that task will definitely fall to her, no question, which is annoying. But when she reasons that everyone else is likely freaking out about these things too, she feels reassured that she is not, for instance, the only mom on this subway car whose husband does not adequately value her emotional labour.

The subway jerks to a halt and the doors open wide, and more people file in to search for a spot, yanking off their hats and mitts in the damp warmth of the cramped car. All the seats are taken by now, and Joy settles into hers more firmly as the standing riders wedge themselves into empty spaces and seize the hand straps overhead. The doors chime and close, and Joy presses her back against the hard, formed plastic as the train hurtles ahead and the emptied-out station blurs outside the window.

Of course she would give up her seat if someone asked. She would do it in a heartbeat, if they really needed it. But there are plenty of people here who are much younger than she is. Also it's hard to read the paper standing up. She opens it again, to a photo of a serious-looking scientist staring into a microscope on one page, and a photo of an ominously vacant classroom on another.

The teachers are already doing work to rule, and a lot of the other parents Joy knows have been complaining about this. Why won't the teachers stay after school anymore for Chess Club and Running Club and Homework Club, they ask each other in hushed but heated voices. The students are suffering because of it. Why do the teachers want the students to suffer?

It all seems very selfish, those parents say, and Joy is trying to reserve judgment because she really likes the teachers at their school. They're doing a good job. But if she's being honest, she is starting to agree with some of the things those other parents are saying. When Joy's daughter went to Homework Club earlier in the school year, she got all of her homework done before she even got home, and that saved everyone so much trouble.

And besides all that, there is this virus in the news, and how is anyone supposed to concentrate on anything else like office work or helping the kids with their homework or even just preparing dinner every night for the family? Which is another thing her husband expects her to do on top of everything else. One of these days she's going to sit him down and have a conversation about dividing up the household tasks more equally. She'll wait until they are both in good moods and not feeling antagonistic toward each other, which she read on the Internet is the best time for that kind of conversation.

Some of the parents are saying that the teachers' unions should wait and see how this virus situation plays out before they go on strike. That would be more considerate of them, they say, and Joy thinks that makes a lot of sense. Okay, yes, the school board shared a letter this week from Public Health saying there are no confirmed cases in Canada so everything's fine, but there's still no need to rush into anything.

And wouldn't it be such a strange and crazy thing for students to wear face masks at school? Like they were in a science-fiction movie, which is Joy's least favourite kind of movie. She doesn't like thinking about aliens invading the Earth, or about sinister future societies that are run by robots.

She flips the page to the Life and Style section, which she always finds comforting because the stories aren't about anything upsetting, and when she reads them she is filled with a warm and lighthearted feeling of well-being.

There is an article about putting together the ultimate beach-resort wardrobe that will take the wearer *from carefree days to hedonistic nights*. There's a roundup of the best red wines for *cozy fireside sipping to beat the January blahs*. There's also a recipe for *Perfect Pound Cake*, which can be made more exotic, it says, by adding a pinch of turmeric. After the list of ingredients, there's a funny editor's note about trying the *turmeric twist* at home, and when she served the pound cake to her husband he thought it was a lemon loaf but when he tasted it, *He was (pleasantly) surprised!*

Joy carefully creases the corner of that page, then looks around her again.

There is a woman sitting across from her who is probably about the same age as Joy and whose hair is always covered by a pretty scarf. Today it's an orange one. The scarf has a specific name, Joy thinks, but she doesn't know what it is. It's often in the news but the word never quite stays in her head.

She sees this woman here almost every Monday to Friday. They always end up in the same car, in nearly the same seats, but the woman gets off a few stops earlier. Joy wonders where she goes when she leaves the train. She also wonders what she does on the weekends. Joy doesn't do anything too exciting on the weekends herself. On Saturdays, she does the laundry and the grocery shopping and maybe flips through a magazine if she's lucky. On Sundays, she gets ready for Monday.

Joy has exchanged smiles with this woman a few times now and has the feeling she's a mother too. She has beautiful white teeth and her skin is the exact colour of the tan Joy has always wanted but has never achieved. The closest Joy has ever come to having skin like hers was the summer when she was sixteen and worked at a go-kart track and she hated every minute of it, but at the end of that summer she had the best tan of her life.

Now she burns so easily and there's skin cancer in her family so she wears SPF 60 or higher. Good luck getting a tan with that stuff all over you.

The main reason Joy thinks the woman is a mom is that she looks so tired. Joy has never spoken to her because if she did, there might suddenly be an obligation to speak to each other all the time, and part of the reason Joy likes her commute is that she doesn't have to talk to anyone. Anyway, if the other woman is a mom, then she probably likes that part too.

Joy wonders what it is about moms and tiredness. She hasn't been sleeping well for a long time now. She either has trouble falling asleep or she wakes up in the middle of the night and can't get back to sleep. She just lies there in the dark bedroom, becoming more and more resentful of her slumbering husband beside her. Glaring at the regular rise and fall of his chest and the occasional soft sighs signalling his happy oblivion. Last night, she woke up because he was breathing on her. His head on his pillow was too close to her head on her pillow and his mouth and nose were only inches away, and she could feel every puff of his exhalations like a knife in her face. She could've just rolled over, but she didn't want to. She wanted him to roll over, but he didn't.

Her doctor recently suggested that her sleep issues might be caused by the onset of perimenopause, but she did not accept that suggestion. She told him that to his face, then left his office without saying goodbye. She had never done that before, and on her way out of the building and through the parking lot to her car, her stride was shaky and her shoulders and jaw were rigid, as if she'd short-circuited. She didn't regret her behaviour, though, because the doctor was wrong. She can't turn her brain off is the problem. She thinks too much about everything. That's all it is.

The woman who is probably a mother too reaches up to touch her scarf. Joy bets it feels silky. Her own pasty hands twitch in her lap while the woman fiddles with the zipper of her coat, and Joy wonders if the fabric of her scarf ever gets caught in there. The woman turns to look at the advertisement behind her seat, and Joy looks at it too.

The advertisement is for a meal-delivery service that promises *Hearty Fare for Those Who Care*. The poster shows a wicker basket overflowing with spaghetti and meatballs in tomato sauce. On the white table below are heart-shaped sauce splatters, which is charming and aggravating all at once.

Joy narrows her eyes at the terrible ad that still somehow makes her feel bad about herself. But then she worries the woman might think she's narrowing her eyes at *her*, so she quickly looks away and remembers how the teenage boys she worked with at the go-kart track would always make a big deal out of shouting, "Hey, everybody, somebody's going on a *Joy Ride*!" whenever she sent a customer off in one of the small, multicoloured race cars. It wasn't a particularly rude thing for them to say, but it still *felt* rude.

All the ads on this subway car, Joy realizes now, are for meal-delivery services. There are so many options to choose from. Takeout food can be delivered to your home from a restaurant. Pre-assembled meal ingredients can be delivered to your home from a supermarket, although in that case you have to cook the meal yourself, which is not ideal.

Joy yawns as they stop inside a tunnel. They are stationary for a while, all of them resting there together in the dark, before the subway car begins to move at a crawl past the grey concrete walls outside the windows. There are dents in the wall like moon craters, and Joy's head slumps so her chin rests on her chest and the colourful ads are dimly reflected in the grey puddles on the floor, and—

There is a company that will deliver sandwiches to your home from a remote location that nobody has ever visited and nobody ever will. It's underground and locked up tight with many, many security protocols in place, and it's populated by robots who will prepare your food lovingly, although these robots have never tasted food themselves and they don't know what love is either.

The robots will stiffly place two slices of the bread of your choice (gluten-free is available) onto the sterile preparation surface. They will add the protein item, cheese (dairy or non-dairy), toppings, and condiments of your choice to the bottom slice of bread. When they press the top slice of bread onto the sandwich fixings, they will light up all over their shiny metal bodies. Because they know it would be so easy for human beings to make these exact same sandwiches themselves. It's not as if the robots are making anything complicated or fancy or gourmet. They're just making sandwiches with basic ingredients that anyone could purchase at a regular grocery store. And yet the humans have chosen to put their faith in the cogs and gears of these hard-working machines, and that makes the robots feel something close to happiness.

When the customer receives their sandwich, maybe they will place it upon a plate and sit down at their dining table to consume it, or maybe they will just eat it straight out of the box because they're so hungry and this sandwich looks so good, and fresh, and as if it was lovingly prepared by other human beings, maybe someone like their grandmother if she had been a kinder person. It definitely doesn't look like it was prepared by robots in a secret underground bunker that no humans will ever see, and they don't have the inclination to see it either, because they've spent such a long day at the office and they have zero leisure time. They can hardly bear to eat it, it's such a work of art, but all they had for lunch was a keto bar at their desk, and it wasn't even one of the sort-of-good-tasting keto bars. It tasted like dust and stuck in their molars all afternoon, to the point where they started to worry that they might lose another filling. They lost a filling last month and had to go to the dentist, and that was not a great experience. The dentist they go to does not have a very nice manner, and once she did not wear gloves when she put her fingers inside their mouth. Afterwards she stared at her bare hands and blinked in a confused way and said, "Oops, look at that. I forgot."

The gentle automated female voice that announces the stops is speaking to Joy and telling her to wake up. "Stop daydreaming about robots, Joy, or you're going to miss your chance."

She opens her eyes and the woman sitting across from her is smiling at her. Watching her with blue eyes bright against light-brown skin. Joy jolts upright and wipes away drool, and her heart hammers as her shaking fingers feel for her purse, and it's there. *Of course it's there, where else would it be?*

Joy's face flushes and she continues to fidget and rummage around, scowling into her bag and extracting a Kleenex that she doesn't actually need. She holds the clean white tissue in her hand for too long and finally crumples it into a soft ball and shoves it back into her purse. She checks to see if the woman is still watching her, but she isn't.

The woman is looking down at her lap and typing something into her phone, and her grin widens and lights up her whole face and now she's looking up again, but not at Joy. Her happy gaze is focused instead on the window behind Joy, on her own reflection in the dark glass.

Joy's cheeks are very hot and she remembers her doctor's lips wiggling around that jagged, slow-motion word—*perimenopause*—but she knows this is not a hot flash. She's just feeling self-conscious.

Once, she and her husband walked through a Black neighbourhood in Brooklyn unexpectedly. One moment they had been surrounded by other white people, and then suddenly they weren't.

Groups of men were lounging on front porches on either side of the street, talking and laughing loudly.

It was a humid night and the air was heavy and they were both sweating, but Joy was wearing a sundress that made her feel good about herself, the peach-coloured one that billowed.

Even when there wasn't a breeze, the fabric was so light that it floated around her bare legs. She'd seen it in a magazine, and the body shape of the woman wearing it on the glossy page looked almost like Joy's body shape, so she'd ordered the dress online immediately.

The men kept laughing, and she was convinced she felt their eyes on her, and she tightened her grasp on her husband's arm.

He pulled away slightly and said, "Why are you grabbing me so hard?"

And she murmured, as quietly as possible so only he could hear, "Because of where we are."

Later, when they were sitting in an air-conditioned restaurant surrounded by people who looked like them again, Jeremy called Joy a racist. She thought he was joking but he wasn't.

It was their fifth wedding anniversary and they didn't have kids yet and they were celebrating with a trip to New York, and this restaurant was supposed to be excellent, but now her stomach was upset and she couldn't even enjoy her shaved pork medallions that had been rolled up to resemble ancient scrolls.

"How can you say that to me?" she asked him.

He said, "Because of how you acted back there."

"But they were *looking* at me," she said.

He shrugged and kept eating.

She wanted to hit him but instead she just pushed her plate away and hissed, "Well, you're not a woman so you don't understand."

He seemed as if he might say something else but he didn't, and her face was hot (all those years ago, see?—she was definitely too young for a hot flash then) and the chair she was sitting on was so uncomfortable because it was made from corrugated metal and the ridges were digging into her and what a stupid design for a chair. But Jeremy had insisted on this place because the reviews were so good, and they had both gotten dressed up and she'd been looking forward to this evening together in an exciting city and now he'd ruined it.

No one had ever called her that word before, and Jeremy was her *husband*, of five years, who had loved her all this time. Sometimes they had arguments and in the middle of them she'd wonder if he still loved her, but by the next day she'd know that he did. Was this an argument? She wasn't sure.

After a period of silence, she went back to her pork scrolls and he ordered them another bottle of wine, and by the next day everything was back to normal. They rode the Staten Island Ferry together and the weather was perfect, and a man who was white but looked homeless asked if they'd like him to take their photo by the Statue of Liberty and Joy said yes immediately, even though his clothes and fingernails were dirty and he was missing some teeth when he smiled.

The subway slows to a stop now and the doors open, and the woman across from her stands up.

And so does Joy, but not until the woman's back is turned and Joy is able to duck behind several other passengers who are also getting out. She stands up so quickly that her newspaper falls off her lap onto the floor and is immediately soaked. She should pick it up. She would normally do that. But this is a new year, she thinks, with new possibilities. Somebody else can do the cleaning-up today.

They all shuffle off the train together in their bulky coats with the farmy smell of wet wool steaming off them and the high-pitched squeaking of boots, with Joy's heart thumping overtop of it all—fast and hard and insistent.

The doors ding and slide shut behind them, and Joy searches the crowd for the woman.

Joy doesn't see her at first and she whacks her thigh with her fist for not paying closer attention, but then she spots the woman's bright orange headscarf bobbing along like a tropical sunset, and her cheeks flare hot-pink again because of that embarrassing comparison—she had actually thought that to herself, in those exact words: *Like a tropical sunset.*

They are all making their slow procession up the stairs now, dripping melted snow and gripping the railing with hands of all sizes and colours nearly touching, then finally reaching the top and breaking apart as everyone veers off in different directions.

Joy follows the woman onto the sidewalk at a discreet distance, allowing a few people to come between them, and keeps as far away as she can without losing sight of her.

The two of them walk along like that for a while, together but separate, and Joy savours the cold air on her warm face as she trudges through the slush in this unfamiliar neighbourhood.

The woman pauses to linger before a storefront window display and then moves on. When Joy passes the same spot, she glances at the decorative arrangement of shiny gift boxes piled behind the shiny glass, leftover from Christmas and probably due for a change soon. Joy's Christmas had been disappointing. Jeremy used to give her such thoughtful presents, but this year he had given her socks and a sub-scription to a cooking magazine.

She and Jeremy don't even watch TV together anymore after the kids have gone to bed. The programs they like are so different. Joy prefers historical dramas and Jeremy is heavily into sci-fi. His favourite show is about an attractive female cyborg bounty hunter who pursues her prey relentlessly and sleeps with them before she kills them. Joy watched an episode with him once and it was ridiculous.

The woman stops again, and so does Joy. The woman cocks her head to the side, and Joy quickly ducks behind a giant inflatable gingerbread man outside a candy store, but thankfully the woman is only taking a moment to adjust her headscarf. Still, to avoid looking suspicious, Joy pulls her cellphone out of her purse and peers at it, furrowing her brow.

The woman bends down in front of a newspaper box and frowns at the headline, which Joy can't see from where she's standing. Then the woman starts walking again at a brisker pace and so does Joy, and she passes the same newspaper box and has the opportunity to read the same words the woman just read, but she doesn't because they're probably about the virus or the school strike or climate change, and she's not interested in any of those topics because she has just noticed the woman's boots.

They are slim and pointed and creamy white, possibly leather, astoundingly fashionable but completely impractical for this season. Joy worries the woman might slip but her steps are sure and steady on the icy pavement, and there are so many things that Joy wants to say to her, such as: *What do you do on the weekends?* And: *Do you have kids, and was your husband more romantic before you had them?* Her mouth silently forms the shape of those sentences, one after the other.

"Why are you following me?" the woman is asking, and Joy blinks at her, skidding to a halt in her own sensible winter boots that protect her feet from the elements and keep them warm and dry. She was so pleased with these boots when she bought them, but now they're so ugly.

"I don't know," Joy mumbles.

"That's not a good answer," says the woman, and her white teeth flash under the dull grey sky, and Joy wonders if she's daydreaming again, if she's mixed up this person in her sleep-deprived brain with a high school teacher who used to tell her that all the time. *That's not a good answer, Joy*, Mrs. Beevis would say in her eternally dissatisfied voice. *I know you can do better*.

But instead she's awake and standing here.

The woman crosses her arms and says, "I don't know you."

"You do!" Joy nods, and the up-and-down movement is frantic, too fast. "It's me, from the subway. We've smiled at each other!" She smiles again now. "I'm Joy."

The woman shakes her head slowly back and forth. "No."

Joy takes a step forward, her hand outstretched, but the woman backs away and shoves open the glass doors of a tall office tower that looks so much like Joy's office tower that she squints at the address, but of course the numbers are different.

The woman throws a final nervous glance over her shoulder before she slips inside and disappears.

Joy stands there, not moving yet, even though she's going to be late for work.

The glass doors are like a mirror, and behind her, on the roof of a taxi, is an illuminated sign advertising a meal-delivery service. The taxi sprays her with slush as it rushes away, but that doesn't even matter.

She's alone with her pale reflection and all the other people on the street, and she doesn't care about any of them.

GARY HOW DOES A CONTACT FORM WORK DO I JUST TYPE IN HERE AND THEN PRESS SEND AND THAT'S IT?

HI THERE! ☺

This isn't something I normally do, so please excuse me if I don't have the etiquette right! But I felt moved to write to you because something hilarious happened to me involving YOU and your TALENTS. Haha. Maybe hilarious isn't the right word. Serendipitous? Possibly. There's one word I'm sure of, though, which is DELICIOUS.

I'll stop being so mysterious! Here's what happened: I found your recipe for Caribbean Style Chickpea Curry With Rice. And…I LOVED IT.

So I wanted to reach out to you, Aliyah (what a pretty name, and so unique! I had to really focus on the spelling when I was copying it out), and tell you that you are helping people. I wanted you to know that. You are shining a very bright light in a very dark time.

Things have gotten so bad that I actually started browsing the self-tanners on Well.ca last night, if you can believe it. Because of course I haven't been able to see my hairdresser to touch up my greys, and being inside so much is totally washing me out. It's awful. You're lucky you don't have to worry about that! So I'm jealous but also thankful because your recipe was like a much-needed dose of tropical sunshine.

I've known how to make a basic curry for a while now. Dice some onions, throw them in a pan with some oil, shake some curry powder on top. After that, though, I'm always looking for inspiration. Up until recently, I only ever searched for East Indian recipes. I am a big East Indian fan! But a few weeks ago, I had a real roti craving. A *chickpea curry* roti, to be exact. ☺

It was already close to dinnertime so I proposed getting takeout, but my husband said my idea was "tricky" because he didn't want roti (not because of the taste but because he's gluten-free). And of course our son Mickey wouldn't touch anything on the menu (yes, his name is Mickey, don't get me started, my husband comes from a family of Disney fanatics so I was under a lot of pressure there, but I didn't have any names I was particularly attached to so I figured why not, and then I regretted it but now it's too late). This is the endless challenge of navigating restaurant meals around the palate of a nine-year-old. Do you have kids? If you do then I'm sure you'll understand how we always have to take Mickey's pickiness into account, and this is why we only ever order food from places where all three of us can find something acceptable to eat.

So basically my husband wanted to save money by not ordering takeout from more than one restaurant. Which was understandable but still frustrating, so I said to him, "Fine, I guess I'll never eat roti again until we all get vaccinated." And he said, "Fine, Vanessa, just get your damn roti then!" Which sounded like he was giving me permission to get the roti, and I didn't like that at all.

My husband is always looking for ways to be economical because just like everybody else we're trying to live on a budget because who knows what the future holds, right? Even with the vaccine on the horizon there is still so much uncertainty, but of course that uncertainty is also why I feel entitled to treat myself once in a while.

But in that moment I just became exhausted from it all. You know those moments when every little thing just grinds you down? So I said, "Forget it, Gary. I'll just make a freezer pizza." Even though I still really wanted a chickpea curry roti.

So we had the freezer pizza because that's something everybody can agree on, and I jazzed up my third of it with some sliced olives, and in the end I wasn't even disappointed. Do you know why? Because while I was waiting for the pizza to cook, I searched my phone for "chickpea curry roti recipes" because I had secretly decided to be resourceful and make it myself! Just the inside part, not the outside part because I think that would be too complicated. But I figured I could do a decent job with the filling if I found the right recipe. And yours was the second or third one that came up and it caught my attention because the photo of the finished dish looked SO GOOD and you also suggested serving it with rice, which I hadn't even thought of but what a great idea. And I clicked on it, and there you were.

It was helpful that you included a photo of yourself so people know your recipe is authentic, because it's hard to tell otherwise. And your smile was so friendly and encouraging.

I was relieved that I already had almost everything I needed in my pantry. Because if I didn't have something, I'd have to wait because we had just stocked up on groceries (not hoarded! Those people are terrible) so we wouldn't be shopping again for a while. The only thing I didn't have was the Scotch bonnet pepper, but I was fine to leave that out. Don't get me wrong, I don't mind spice. I'm as spicy as they come! Haha, not really. But if the spice is so hot that it masks the other flavours of the dish, that always seems like a waste to me. Once I got a takeout falafel that was so spicy I had to throw it out. I had specified "spice level medium" to the girl when she asked me (they had their own classification system) and I swear she added extra hot sauce on purpose. It felt spiteful. Or maybe that's just what spice level medium means at that restaurant, who knows. But it was so hot that it burned my mouth and I had to spit it out right there on the street, which was upsetting. Oh, and your recipe also called for

"Jamaican curry powder" but I didn't have that so I just used regular curry powder.

The next day I made your Caribbean Style Chickpea Curry With Rice for my dinner (Mickey and his dad ate hot dogs) and let me tell you, the results of my efforts were nothing less than "restaurant quality," which is how my husband and I describe home-cooked food that exceeds our usual standards and we can actually close our eyes and imagine that a professional chef made it for us and a professional server served it to us.

I miss going to restaurants.

Anyway, I thought to myself, *I need to tell this young woman what a positive impact she's had on my life!* So here I am.

I noticed that you're asking people who enjoyed your recipes to give them a star rating, but I can't figure out how to do that. Do I have to create an account? I don't like creating accounts. We're expected to create accounts for everything these days! But then I went to your About Me page and saw the option to email you via this contact form, so I thought I would do that instead because it's more personal.

My friend Melanie recently commented that one good thing about the pandemic is that more people are cooking at home now. Because they have more time on their hands and they can't go to restaurants and they're sick of getting takeout all the time. So now they're embracing home cooking and learning new culinary skills that will last them the rest of their lives. She didn't say that to me directly, she said it on social media. But it still resonated. Mel is an excellent cook, you should follow her. She's my go-to for fusion food. She does her own twists on all sorts of cultural dishes and makes them even better. There are a few Chef Melanies on there, but she's the one with the photo of her baby wearing an apron as her profile picture. Which is funny because obviously the apron is too big and the expression on his chubby pink face is like, "Get this thing off of me!" Haha. At least I think it's her baby.

So you should know that you're doing a wonderful thing, Alliya. You're educating and empowering people by expanding our mealtime repertoires!

Quick suggestion: You might want to consider including a glossary of terms on your site to make it more user-friendly. I had to look up Scotch bonnet peppers and Jamaican curry powder, for instance. But I am no website expert! Technology and I are not BFFs. Haha.

Here's another thing I wanted to tell you: I have become aware.

I've read a number of enlightening books and articles recently, and the effect of reading those books and articles is that one morning, about a month ago, I woke up and felt as if a switch had been pulled in my life. My eyes had been opened to the harsh reality of the world around me and the rotten systems at work within it, and how those systems exclude people and they're so damaging. I blinked and looked around and it was like: Here is this system and I'm a part of it *and I didn't even know*.

A core-shaking realization, to say the least. As if living in the shadow of COVID-19 wasn't disruptive enough! Suddenly the ground was no longer solid beneath me. Up was down and down was up. It was as if a voice was whispering in my ear: "Here's what you knew before, Vanessa, and all of it was wrong." This is what it felt like: it felt like I was living in *The Matrix*. I only saw that movie once and I don't remember the details very well, but people frequently use it as an analogy for this kind of thing and now I know why.

My newly dawning understanding left nothing untouched by its rays. Gary and Mickey and I went to Magic Kingdom last summer with Gary's entire extended family, and against my better judgment we all wore the ears and matching #DisneySquad T-shirts with our names on them.

It was a birthday celebration for Gary's mom and she's a difficult personality so I just went along with it. But I drew the line when Gary wanted to buy a hoodie that said Will Trade Wife For FastPass+ and I told him no way.

I'm telling you all of this because I have a confession to make: my favourite attraction was the Jungle Cruise ride. I loved it. It was so hot out and I was grateful to escape into the cool, soothing shade of the boat. I was tired and sweaty and Mickey was overstimulated and whiny and Gary had been getting on my nerves all day, but for those seven blissfully untroubled minutes, I was happy. We floated together along the dirty, manufactured river and gazed at the animatronic scenes and I loved every single second of it. And our skipper was so clever with his puns! Gary and I laughed so hard! But we shouldn't have, and I know that now.

But thinking back, I can clearly recall a deep and comforting sense of nostalgia that overcame me when I was relaxing in that imitation safari barge surrounded by all of Gary's sunburned relatives. I even remember sighing, that feeling was so strong. I mentioned it to Gary the other day and he said, "Look out, Vanessa, your colonialist roots are showing!" And I said what does that mean, and he said he didn't know, he just thought it sounded smart when stupid Keith at the office said it to him when Gary was talking about missing *Gilligan's Island*.

Anyway, I suspect that feeling I had was only because I went to Magic Kingdom on a family trip to Orlando when I was eight.

Do you have a lot of small scars from all the cooking you do? I bet the answer is yes.

The other day, I accidentally grated myself on the cheese grater. It was sitting there in the sink and I reached in to get something else and then I was in pain, and I looked at my hand and saw that I'd grated some skin off of one of my knuckles, ouch!

Also I wanted to ask your advice about something.

The first time I made your Caribbean Style Chickpea Curry With Rice, it turned out perfectly, as I mentioned. But the second time I made it, the curry was bitter. This has happened to me with curry recipes before, many times, and part of the reason why I was so excited about your recipe was because I thought I'd found the key to avoiding that bitterness forever. But it wasn't.

Maybe you have never had this problem.

You said to brown the onions until they were caramelized and I did that both times. You said to add the spices in a specific order and I followed that order exactly both times. You said to stir the spices over medium heat for just a few minutes so they wouldn't burn, and then to add the can of coconut milk and the can of chickpeas and bring everything to a boil, and I did that both times too. Maybe I burned the spices. But I don't think so. Because I was careful.

Because I learn from my mistakes, and I've gotten pretty good at following recipes over the years. And when I made your dish the first time, everything was in perfect harmony. All the ingredients worked so well together and none of them shouted too loudly over the others. But the second time, I was full of anticipation and I did everything you said I should do, but the desired result was not achieved.

I googled "How do you fix a bitter curry?" and found some tips but none of them helped. I tried adding a pinch of sugar and then a pinch of salt. I tried adding extra coconut milk, and then some yogurt, and then a few squeezes of fresh lime. But that just made it worse.

Is there a secret you could let me in on? Some secret knowledge that maybe you learned from your mother or your grandmother that you could pass along? Don't be like those selfish panic buyers who stockpile all the hand sanitizer and toilet paper, Alliyia! It's better to share. We're all in this together!

Maybe I should just give up now. But I don't want to. There has to be a special trick with the balancing of the spices and I would really love to know that trick.

Or maybe my spices are stale? I haven't replaced them in a while. I've been avoiding the Bulk Barn because it doesn't seem like the safest place to go these days, with everyone touching all the scoops. Or maybe only the people who work there touch the scoops. I don't know, I'm just staying away for the time being.

Maybe I should find a Caribbean supermarket and buy my spices there? I bought some chai tea at an East Indian supermarket once, though, and it was underwhelming. Also the cashier was a bit rude and said I shouldn't say "East Indian" anymore, and when I asked her why not, her explanation didn't make any sense at all.

What am I doing wrong? Please tell me.

This is a really long email. I wonder if you'll read the whole thing. I hope you do because I'm really looking forward to your reply! ☺

MISTER ELEPHANT

MY FORMER FRIEND is an elephant tamer.

I hadn't seen her in a long time. But then one day, I took my kid to the zoo, and there she was. My kid wanted an elephant ride as soon as she realized that was a thing she could do. I saw her eyes light up with the glorious possibility of it.

I said no.

Because it had been years, and here was my former friend looking so professional and poised in her khaki uniform. And then there was me, wearing my baggy jeans and wiping my kid's runny nose with the back of my hand because I forgot to pack Kleenex, like I always do.

Back in high school, my former friend used to wear a belt tied too high around her body, like she didn't know anything about belt-tying or maybe it was on purpose to make some sort of anti-fashion statement, but in any case, it looked stupid and people made fun of her for it. Now she was saying stuff like, "Line up right here, folks. This is the place for lining up." And people were listening to her and following her instructions.

Back in high school, she used to sit by herself in the cafeteria. Once I saw one of the popular girls walk over and spray her half-empty juice box onto my former friend's lunch so she couldn't eat it anymore. She always used to eat things that didn't make any sense to the rest of us. And now here she was, acting confident and authoritative in her form-fitting outfit and appearing generally satisfied with where she was in life, and very at ease around this gigantic mammal that could've easily squashed her spine with one misplaced foot. But it was probably kinder to her than the jerks in high school had ever been.

My kid started crying and I told her to calm down. I said, "Do you want to see the lemurs? Let's go see the lemurs."

But she said no.

Even with those big, inquisitive eyes? Even with those long, stripey tails?

She wasn't interested. She's never cared about the small, adorable things that little girls are supposed to like, which I've always thought is strange. But I'm trying to focus on my daughter's uniqueness and consider her own specific needs.

The other day I said to her mother, "She doesn't play with dolls. She isn't very nurturing."

And her mother said to me, "You're talking about a societal construct. You're talking about a cage that girls and boys no longer have to be trapped in."

My wife never used to talk like that before, but she's been reading a lot of articles on the Internet lately. They're not just about parenting either. The other night she asked me to do things to her in bed that made me feel uncomfortable. Not the things themselves, just the way she asked for them.

"I hate lemurs, Daddy," said my daughter.

And I thought, *Whoa.*

I wiped her tears and snot with the back of my hand and said, "Let's go get a funnel cake," which was at least something I knew we could agree on.

"Elephant ride! Elephant ride!" she kept shouting.

But she was out of luck there.

And not because my wife said elephant rides are cruel. When I told her we were going to the zoo, she couldn't believe they still have elephant rides here. She said that just proves how crappy our small-town zoo is, and that she wasn't coming with us out of protest. And I said fine, stay home and text your boring office buddies on a Saturday, I don't care. And she said it's not texting, it's called Slack, and she said she was happy to engage with her co-workers on the weekend because her work was meaningful and fulfilling, and that I should enjoy the zoo because the animal-rights activists would probably be shutting it down soon, anyway.

I know she just wants to text with Wayne, who I never liked when I worked there and I like him even less now. My wife can't mention his name without saying his parents are from Mainland China. Like she's all enlightened because she asked him where his family was from and I never bothered, and suddenly she thinks she's better than me because she's buying our groceries at the T&T while I'm still shopping at the Superstore. She told me Wayne wants to come over sometime and show her how to make pork dumplings, and I said oh yeah, like a private lesson? And she looked down at her hands and said no, you could learn too. But I said I didn't want to. So who knows, maybe they're doing that right now.

Anyway, we're not doing the elephant ride because I don't want to.

I ordered a funnel cake and a Diet Coke, and the man behind the counter gave my kid a big smile and asked her if she wanted ice cream and cherries on top. Then he winked at me for some reason, and I didn't like that. Did he expect me to wink back? What were we supposed to be winking about?

I said, "Don't put anything on it. She doesn't like when it gets all soggy."

"Not even the powdered sugar?" he said.

My kid stared up at me and whispered, "Sugar."

"Okay," I said. "Put the sugar on it."

He winked again, and I wanted to punch him.

Fucking perverted concession seller at the zoo.

Then he said to me, "Guys like us gotta stick together."

At first I didn't know what he was talking about because he had an ugly face and curly orange hair like a clown's, so

I didn't see the similarity. But then I saw him giving the stink-eye to an Asian family, a mom and a dad and two kids all laughing and joking together as they left the picnic area, and I figured it out.

Fucking racist perverted concession seller at the zoo.

There were a bunch of picnic tables and I picked the one that was farthest away from him, even though it had a pile of used napkins on it.

My kid frowned at the napkins and I told her, "People are pigs."

Then she ate her funnel cake and I drank my Diet Coke, and I thought about how I used to drink regular pop. That's all I ever drank. But now my wife says the regular pop is unhealthy.

The sun shone down and my kid and I sat there together, and I thought about all the times I was nice to my former friend and all the times she pretended to be nice back to me.

As if I didn't know she was faking it.

Because I was the only one in our entire high school who would sit next to her at lunch. We'd sit together and she'd eat her eel-head soup or crab pie or fried pig intestines and I'd pretend not to notice the smell like a gentleman while I talked to her about novels I'd read or movies I'd seen or paintings I'd looked at, and how none of them were any good. And of course all art is subjective and a matter of individual taste and preference, and yes I had high standards, but come on, wasn't it bizarre that so much creative work that was supposedly popular and got all this acclaim was in fact nothing special at all? And she would mostly just listen and not say very much back to me, but that's the way some friendships are. They're uneven.

She should've been more grateful, though.

Once she wasn't sitting in her regular spot and I had to search the whole cafeteria until eventually I found her up on the stage behind the curtain where the drama geeks usually sat. I guess since her lunch was extra stinky that day. I was starving by that point so I just said hi and sat down next to her on the hard wooden floor, and started eating my sandwich without a word of complaint. And she didn't even look happy to see me, at least not right away.

A peacock was strutting around nearby. It let out a terrible scream, and I remembered being seven years old and not being able to make a picture out of dots. Which might seem like a weird way to be reminded of something, but my daughter is turning seven next year. And lots of things remind me of that memory because I'm always thinking about it.

During that art lesson, the teacher told us to close our eyes and make tiny pencil marks all over our pieces of paper. We were supposed to do that for five minutes, and then we could open our eyes and an image would magically appear.

It never worked for me, but it always worked for this one boy in our class. The teacher would ooh and ahh over his pencil-dot renderings of trees and rainbows and cars and army tanks and dragons and robots, and hold them up for the rest of us to admire. "Look at this," she'd say. "Feast your eyes on what is possible."

They really weren't that great, though. You couldn't always tell what the object was right away. Sometimes you had to squint to see it.

The teacher only made a big deal out of that kid's assignments because she felt sorry for him. She told us during a geography lesson that he was born in another country where all sorts of inequality and intolerance happened. Then his mother brought him here to enjoy and benefit from all the equality and tolerance in our country. On a giant map of the world, the teacher used her pointer to jab at Cambodia, and then she drew an imaginary heart around Canada. "Our homes have similar names, don't they?" she said to the class. "But they're very, very different." She smiled at the boy and asked if he had anything to add. And he mumbled something about a pen because he was probably trying to redirect the conversation back to art, and the teacher smiled more and said, "Yes, you're right! Pens are plentiful here!" She was always giving him praise when he didn't deserve it.

The peacock screamed again. It was too close to us so I shooed it away.

"Why is that fancy bird making those scary sounds?" said my daughter. Her mouth was all white with icing sugar. "He sounds like he's in pain."

"Keep eating," I told her. "You're almost done."

I stopped thinking about the boy and I went back to thinking about my former friend.

I first noticed her in Grade 9 biology class when she gave a presentation on South American wildlife. I can't remember if elephants were included but I do remember being captivated by her accent. I liked the softness of it. So when we were paired up as lab partners, I was excited.

She said she was from Chile and I asked if it was really cold there, haha, and she said no. She told me that her dream was to work with animals someday, and I told her I used to want to be an artist but not anymore. Not for a long time, actually.

She said if I wanted to be an artist, I should be an artist. That I should believe in myself and follow my dreams while I still could because you never know, one day everything could change. She gazed at me very intensely, and then we dissected a frog together, and I thought to myself, *She could be my wife one day*.

For a long time I was fully convinced that would happen, but it didn't. Life is full of surprises.

Here's another example. For years I worked in the same office with the same men and women and we never really socialized, until we started having group lunches to honour our fellow employees' birthdays. Everybody from the various departments would sit together at one long table and there would be a balloon tied to the chair of the person who was having the birthday. And the first time we did that, the person we were celebrating was a woman I'd never noticed before. That night I ended up at her house. She had a big, decorative frame on one wall of her bedroom, and the only thing inside the frame was one word: *Laugh*. As if it was a command or something. I didn't like that, but I slept with her anyway.

Then she got pregnant and then we got married, and then I got laid off but she didn't, and she still works at the same office with the same people who ask how I'm doing all the time, and I hate that.

"People today can be anything they want to be," my wife likes to say. But if that was true, the world would be better.

My kid's plate was empty and she started stabbing the Styrofoam with her plastic fork. She did that for a while, then stopped and said, "Look, Daddy, I made a dinosaur!"

I didn't really see it, but I told her she did a good job. There was a hump-shaped line of dots at the top that could've been the body, and a longer line of dots on one side that could've been the tail or the neck. She hadn't closed her eyes, though, so it didn't count.

"Put that in the garbage now," I told her. "We need to clean up our mess."

And she listened to me. She picked up the plate and the fork and even the napkins that somebody else had left there and she threw them all away.

I crumpled my can and looked around for a recycling bin, and when I couldn't find one, I stuck it in my pocket to recycle at home because I'm a responsible adult with a family now.

I'm a father, and fathers are important.

"Come on," I said to my daughter. "There's somebody I want you to meet."

"Who?" she said.

I winked at her. "I think his name is Mister Elephant."

And she squealed, which was so cute, and she jumped and twirled for me like a ballerina and I couldn't have been prouder.

She held my hand and skipped the whole way over, and I even skipped a little too, because I had a good feeling that maybe things were about to change.

AVALANCHE

TINA IS LOOKING FORWARD TO attending the Women's March
tomorrow with her daughter. Ashley was too young for the
first one last year, but now she's six, old enough to stand
still for some speeches and then walk slowly for possibly up
to forty-five minutes in the cold without (too much) complaining, so that she'll get to see all the strong, empowered
women around her and feel empowered too.

Tina has told her, "Most of them will be happy, but some
of them might be angry. But don't worry. Anger can be a
good thing, sometimes."

She even made Ashley her own little sign to wear.

She is a bit disappointed that she couldn't find hats for
them. Ashley would've looked so cute (and so would Tina!)
in one of those knitted pink kitty-ear hats. Tina searched all
over but none of the stores she normally shops at carried
them. She doesn't like shopping online because she never
knows when the package will arrive. Once she ordered an
artisanal snow globe online and the box came in the evening while she and Brian were watching TV. The delivery
interrupted one of Brian's favourite shows right at a really
suspenseful part, and he wasn't pleased about that.

Tina is pondering all of this as she rinses the dirty breakfast dishes. Then she puts them in the dishwasher and thinks,
"Ashley" is an outdated name. This is a thought she has often,
especially when she's alone in the house. Brian goes to work
and Ashley goes to school and Tina stays home and cleans
up after them, which is her job and she's glad to do it, but
there is still a wave of discontent that builds because she

has never stopped being upset with herself for not giving her daughter a better name. Something classic but unique. Ashley is a name from the 1990s, which was when Tina went to high school and the prettiest girl in her grade was named Ashley. Tina thought then—and continued to think even in her late thirties, when she met Brian and was relieved to find he didn't have any baby names he was particularly attached to—*That's what I'm going to call my daughter one day*.

And then they had Ashley, and now she's six and the Women's March is tomorrow, and Tina is wishing she'd chosen a bolder and more assertive name such as "Artemis" or "Zora," like the moms of a couple of girls in Ashley's Grade 1 class did.

Tina often feels in awe of the originality of those moms and also their forward thinking, because suddenly so many bold and assertive women who look a lot like Tina but who are so much braver are getting together on the Internet and sharing very personal stories about how different men have hurt them in different ways, all throughout their lives. And now some of these men are losing their jobs and others are just being humiliated on social media. When it all started, Brian said things like, "Wow, there sure are a lot of creeps in the world," but lately he's been saying things like, "How far do you think this is going to go? I mean, I get it, but where does it stop?" And Tina never has an answer for him because she has a lot of feelings about all of this, but none of them make any sense to her.

But she felt good about making the sandwich-board sign for Ashley with pink string and neon-pink bristol board that reads "I AM A SNOWFLAKE" in bold bubble letters on the front, and on the back it reads "TOGETHER WE ARE AN AVALANCHE!!"

She started working on it yesterday morning after she dropped Ashley off at school because she was inspired by a chance encounter. Tina believes in serendipity because if it isn't real, how can anyone explain the way Brian chose her out of all the other options available on the dating site they were both on? And how did she end up giving birth to the daughter who is exactly like the one she always envisioned when she used to dream about having a daughter?

What happened was, on her walk back home from the school, she passed a woman who was taking big, confident strides on the icy sidewalk in impractical pointy boots, and the woman was wearing headphones and singing along in a very loud voice to whatever music she was listening to. Tina could hear almost every word but she didn't recognize the tune. The woman was off-key but she boomed the song out anyway, and her enthusiasm made Tina feel sweaty and embarrassed for her, even though the woman didn't seem to care that she wasn't a good singer. Or maybe she didn't even know.

When she was a kid, Tina used to think she was a great singer and imagined she might even grow up to sing professionally. One day she recorded herself with her tape deck singing along to Wham! on her Walkman with her headphones on, and she was eager to hear what she sounded like without the musical accompaniment. But when she played back her voice singing all by itself, it was horrible. Maybe this woman had never done that, Tina reasoned, so she still thought she sounded way better than she actually did.

When Tina got home, though, she headed straight upstairs to the office and switched on the family computer. First she found the video for "Everything She Wants" on YouTube. She hovered over the small white triangle and then clicked it hard, and the room filled with the tap-tap-tapping of cymbals that always made her heart beat a little faster, and then came George Michael's smooth, plaintive vocals. She jerked up the volume and sang along at the top of her voice while she googled "women's march protest sign sayings," and by the end of the song, she'd found the perfect one.

Then she googled "How do you make a protest sign?" because she had some ideas but maybe they weren't the right ones.

She made a list on her phone of what she needed and pictured herself and Ashley standing tall and marching together against injustice, and then she went to the Dollar Store.

This year, this march, was going to be special for her and Ashley. They couldn't even watch more than five minutes of the first Women's March from home last year because the TV broke. But tomorrow the two of them would go, in person, to this gathering that had been organized to affirm that the world was indeed a good place for women and girls to live in. Because it was important for Ashley to see that, and for Tina to be there with her when she did.

She purchased all the protest-sign materials and brought everything home and got to work right away. She punched holes in the bristol board and attached the string, and when she wrote out the uplifting phrase in black felt marker, she added two exclamation marks at the end because of how exhilarated those words made her feel.

Last night, when Ashley was finally asleep (it takes a long time for that to happen these days—a lot of reading and talking and lullabying has to happen first, but Tina doesn't mind), Tina decided to draw a snowflake on Ashley's protest sign with a blue glitter-glue pen instead of watching Brian's zombie show with him. She was feeling pretty proud of how it was looking, even though she was also remembering the article she'd read recently about how scientists wanted to ban glitter because it was killing ocean life, so she really shouldn't buy it anymore.

And then Brian said, "People are going to take pictures of her, you know."

By which, Tina knew, he meant men.

So then Tina thought maybe Ashley shouldn't wear her small but significant protest sign. That made Tina feel defeated, but also like a good mom because she was looking out for her daughter and keeping her safe. Because without her neon-pink sign, Ashley would be more likely to blend into the background and not draw the attention of people looking to take photos of cute kids wearing interesting protest signs, and also creepy men using the Women's March as an excuse to take photos of women and girls they wanted to think perverted thoughts about later.

On the screen, two zombies were disembowelling somebody who was still alive, and the victim thrashed and screamed while the pale hands ripped and tore, and Tina looked away. She hated Brian's zombie show, but he got upset when she complained about it.

In the back of her mind, though, Tina had also been thinking that the sign's bright colour would help her keep track of Ashley in the crowd. She wasn't planning on letting go of her hand, ever. But let's say Ashley tried to run away from her at some point—something Ashley has threatened to do in the past and has never done in reality, but there's always a first time. In that case, blending into the background would be a bad thing.

On TV, the victim was on the ground and she kicked her legs, and her feet connected with one zombie's chest and he fell backwards. Tina cheered silently until the other zombie picked up a big rock and hit the victim on the head with it. Then a commercial for aftershave came on and Brian made the cute face that meant he wanted a blow job, so she gave him one.

Tina doesn't worry about creepy men being interested in her anymore. She's in her early forties now, and zero scary male strangers have whistled or yelled anything crude at her for a long time. But she worries for Ashley, whose beauty takes Tina's breath away sometimes. She often wishes her daughter was plain and unremarkable, like Tina has always been. There is some protection in that.

Even now, at six years old, Ashley has nightmares about bad men trying to get her. Tina used to wonder where that fear came from, but then Ashley told her that she plays Bad Man with her friends at school. Her friend Eloise made it up. It's their favourite game, apparently. The boys take turns being the Bad Man and they chase the girls to the back of the schoolyard, and the girls all try to stay together because if one of them gets separated, the Bad Man will tie that girl to the fence with a scarf and do things to her.

"What kinds of things?" Tina asked Ashley when she first told her that, but Ashley just shrugged and said she was too fast for the boys to catch her, and Tina was relieved.

"Eloise" is a classic name, but still unique. It also means "famous warrior"—Tina looked it up. The meaning of "Ashley" is "dweller near the ash tree forest," which is disappointing.

Thankfully, Brian is the best man that Tina has ever known. When they first started dating, being with him felt like bouncing her old red-white-and-blue rubber ball against the side of her house every summer and sledding on her little red toboggan down the gently sloped hill in the park every winter. Being Brian's girlfriend, and then his wife, reminded her of how she and her friends used to run away squealing from the neighbour's Rottweiler and hide in her garage. The dog would scratch and growl at the door, and Tina and the other kids would scream louder and louder and that was fun, but she also always wondered where her parents were and why they weren't rushing over to shoo the dog away. Brian would've rescued her, though, if they'd known each other then. He would've grabbed that dog by its wide, muscular neck and forced it down on the driveway until it knew he was the boss, and then it would have run away and never come back.

Plus, all the men before Brian made Tina feel awful about herself. But then she found him, and together they made Ashley, and things are so much better now.

Or they were, until Tina started learning about rape culture and not really understanding it but then sort of understanding it, and reading all these stories in the news about women accusing men of horrible things and not-so-horrible things. The whole point was that anyone was allowed to say, "Me too," even someone like Tina, who has nothing much to complain about.

Everything is getting more complicated now and Tina doesn't like it. She knows she's supposed to teach Ashley about rape culture, but she doesn't know how. She could get a book about it from the library, but there are so many books to choose from. She could look up answers on the Internet, but how would she know if those answers were the right ones? People have a lot of opinions on the Internet.

Tina isn't even sure if it's okay to enjoy rough sex anymore. She has never been raped, so how dare she? Brian says she shouldn't think so much about everything because it ruins the mood. So she tries to shut off her brain and let herself feel everything he's doing to her, but sometimes that's not a good idea either.

Anyway, she's looking forward to the Women's March. It's been a brutal winter, but this weekend the weather is supposed to co-operate.

The wind howls outside and Tina is glad to be inside folding the laundry, which is warm from the dryer. She only misses her old job sometimes. She misses the plants that made the office feel sort of tropical. After she quit, she tried to recreate that same environment at home, but then everything died. The plants at the office were all so lush and green and healthy-looking because somebody else took care of them.

She doesn't miss the commute and she doesn't miss the actual work, which was boring and repetitive. But she misses the plants, and she misses her co-workers. But mostly just Donna.

"Do you know something I just realized?" Donna said to Tina once, when they were both in the break room getting coffee and it was just the two of them. "You and I are basically the same person."

They stood there smiling at each other in their matching separates, which they hadn't even coordinated beforehand, and how awesome was that? Tina had arrived that morning wearing a yellow blouse and a yellow cardigan with navy-blue slacks, and Donna was already at her desk, wearing *the exact same outfit*.

"Do you really think so?" Tina asked her, because she very much wanted to believe in the truth of this marvellous thing that her cubicle mate had just proclaimed.

Donna nodded as she shook a bunch of non-dairy powdered creamer into her mug. "I do," she said, and stirred vigorously.

Tina watched Donna's black coffee turn beige, and the great magnitude of that small action was not lost on her. She gazed at the miniature whirlpool that Donna was creating with her little plastic stir stick and saw a future where all good things were achievable. *I'm white, and Donna is Black*, she thought, feeling her chest swell with momentousness. *And together, we can accomplish anything*.

They headed back to their desks then, and resumed their data entry.

Tina pulls another pair of Brian's briefs out of the dryer and folds them neatly before placing them in the hamper.

When Tina's tiny tadpole daughter was swimming around inside her and it was still too early to share the shining news of her existence with anyone, the only person Tina really wanted to tell was Donna, but she never did. Tina's parents would've been the other people, but they had both died of heart attacks the year before she met Brian.

On Tina's last day at the office—which happened soon after the positive pregnancy test because Brian was so excited about the baby that he wanted Tina to stop working right away, not for maternity leave but forever—Donna brought Tina a doughnut from the café in the basement of their building and frowned when she said their manager should've given Tina a farewell party.

Tina said Katie P. probably didn't have enough time to plan. Then she ate the doughnut, which was delicious.

Donna shook her head in a slow and significant way. "No, two weeks is plenty of time."

But it wasn't, not for Tina. The days after she gave her notice sped by and then they were gone, and so was Donna.

Tina regularly wishes she could have Donna over for coffee or tea or even wine—wouldn't that be fun!—but even if she had Donna's contact information, she could never have her over because the house is filled with embarrassing souvenirs from the all-inclusive resort in Jamaica where Tina and Brian went for their honeymoon.

It was a nice vacation but also not nice, and now Tina can never forget it because all their fridge magnets are either flip-flops or rum bottles or sunset silhouettes of two dolphins kissing, a set of their wineglasses are made from coconut shells, and a set of their mugs are red and yellow and green with slogans on them such as "One Love" and "Everyting Irie."

There's also a pair of glossy wooden maracas that say "Jamaican Me Crazy!" in a ceramic bowl on their dining room table, which Ashley tried to play with once but Brian told her no, they were just decorative. To make Ashley feel better, the next day Tina bought her two little musical shakers shaped like eggs, which Tina thought were cute, but Ashley wasn't interested in them.

Worst of all is the Rasta wig attached to the colourful knitted cap that hangs on a hook in the master bedroom, and any time there's a breeze from the window, the imitation dreadlocks shake like they're alive. Sometimes Brian puts it on and says, "No problem, mon!" to make Tina and Ashley laugh, even though that behaviour isn't funny at all. But they laugh anyway.

Tina isn't comfortable with any of it, but the one time she tried to hide the souvenirs in a closet, Brian really got into a mood. So now she leaves them where they are.

Tina is vacuuming now, back and forth across the carpet in the TV room. How did she ever find time for these tasks when she used to spend her days creating spreadsheets and populating them with numbers that meant nothing to her? One last stubborn crumb disappears into the machine's roaring mouth, and the floor is clean. Taking care of her family means something, she tells herself. She switches off the vacuum and sighs.

Brian is right about Ashley's protest sign. Of course he is. It's not a good idea.

She goes to the place in the dining room where she has propped the sign against a wall in the far corner, out of everyone's way but ready for action. She picks it up and lays it on the table, then tears open the two holes she'd punched in at the top and removes the two loops of string. Now the two pieces of bristol board are separate again, and she tucks them under her arm and tosses the string into the kitchen trash can before heading for the recycling bin in the garage.

Because string doesn't go in recycling, and one of her biggest pet peeves is when people don't dispose of waste properly. What is wrong with those people? They're all living on the same planet, which will die if they don't take care of it, and it's the easiest thing in the world to figure out what goes in the garbage and the recycling and the green bin. That's at least one small step toward improving things, and yet so many idiots just can't be bothered.

Brian says she shouldn't worry so much about the environment because what's the point. He says they'll both be dead by the time the Earth explodes, anyway. She knows he's probably right. But once she woke him up in the middle of the night and whispered, "But what about Ashley?"

And he shrugged and rolled on top of her and said, "Then stop using so much hairspray."

Tina dumps the snowflake sign into the recycling bin and it sparkles in the dim, flickering garage light. Now she isn't sure if the sign can be recycled after all, because of the glitter glue she used.

One time at work, Donna told Tina that her daughter Simone used so much glitter in the crafts she made that it was starting to appear in the family's poop, and Tina laughed so hard that she snorted right at her desk.

Donna was laughing hard too. "Marcus came out of the bathroom the other morning and said to me, 'You want to see proof I'm turning into a unicorn?'"

They both lost all control then, until Wanda from Accounts Payable shushed them from two cubicles away.

Tina loved Donna's stories about her family. She remembers all of them.

She could try to connect with Donna on Facebook, but Brian says social media is frivolous and addictive and the companies steal your personal information, and Tina knows that's true. She imagines Ashley being a teenager or even a preteen and living her life online with all the cyberbullies and cyberpredators, and then she has to stop imagining that because it's terrible. The sudden, crushing reality of that future world is at odds with the way she has always tried to frame the present world for herself and her daughter. She had a Facebook account before she got married, but she hasn't checked it in years.

She transfers the protest sign from the recycling bin to the garbage can, then goes back inside to put the laundry away.

She lugs the full basket into Ashley's room first.

The laundry piles up so quickly, every day. Even with all these clean clothes to put away, there are still more dirty clothes in Ashley's hamper. One long sleeve of a discarded pyjama top hangs over the plastic rim, a limp arm dangling in a failed attempt to escape. She could fix it, but she doesn't.

She pulls folded dresses and T-shirts and pairs of leggings and underwear and socks from the stack and finds a home for each item in Ashley's dresser, which her daughter has decorated with puffy cartoon cat stickers. Every so often, when Tina is watching her and also probably when she isn't, Ashley will press a finger gently against each sticker and say, "Purr."

Tina knows about sweatshops and it makes her sad to think about them.

But what is she supposed to do, exactly? She has her own child to take care of. Does she think Ashley is somehow more precious than the young girls who work in the factories in India, making the cheap clothes she feels embarrassed about buying at Walmart? Of course not.

No, that's a lie.

There is a part of her that does think Ashley is more precious, and she hates that part of herself.

But tomorrow will be about empowerment.

She tucks away the last little pair of socks, then stands quietly contemplating the heap of Brian's underwear.

Something else Tina liked about Donna was that she didn't pry. That was always a relief because Tina never had any exciting stories of her own to tell.

She talks to Ashley now, though, when they're alone.

Ashley likes to say hello to all the trees they pass on their walks to and from school. She stops and places her small palm against the rough bark of every trunk and says in a solemn voice, "You are my favourite." Tina has to budget extra time for this, but she doesn't mind. So she holds her daughter's hand and they walk and stop at every tree, and Tina speaks in general terms about Mother Nature and how everyone on Earth has the responsibility to be kind to her and protect her, and Ashley nods with her eyes open wide.

Tina doesn't want to scare her, but she knows that now is the beginning of Ashley's understanding of things, and if she doesn't explain how the world works, then her daughter will fill in the blanks herself.

She finishes with the laundry, then stands in the middle of her and Brian's bedroom waiting to feel a sense of accomplishment.

Suddenly it's snowing. The flurries blur the neighbours' houses and a fierce gust of wind rattles the windowpanes. The blizzard is a deluge of white that obscures everything else.

The only thing left to do is the dusting, but this is Tina's least favourite chore because it includes Brian's souvenirs.

She can pinpoint the exact moment when she started seeing them differently. It was the day Katie P. walked around the office showing off the tan she'd gotten at an all-inclusive five-star island getaway with her husband and kids. They'd gone to Trinidad and Tobago, the same place where Donna had told Tina she went every year to visit relatives.

When their manager arrived at Donna and Tina's cubicle, she waggled her newly bronzed arms in the air and proclaimed, "Oh my God, Donna, I had the BEST Caribbean food at the resort. I tried doubles and they were SO GOOD! I'm totally addicted now." Then her voice went low and conspiratorial. "Can you recommend any good places where I can get my fix? Haha."

Donna didn't look away from her screen. She didn't stop typing. She just shook her head and said, "No."

After Katie P. walked away, Tina wanted to ask her friend if she was okay, and what doubles were, but she never did.

Tina hasn't told Brian about the change in how she feels about all of his Jamaica mementos. He never changes the way he feels about things and she likes that about him, mostly. It's something she can count on.

She roams the house with her microfibre cloth until everything shines.

At the resort on their honeymoon, the sun had been relentless and Tina was always squinting, even when she was wearing sunglasses. She slathered herself with sunscreen and hid in the shade of umbrellas and palm trees while her new husband's skin turned pink and then red, then blistered and peeled off in strips, which made him irritable.

But that's only part of it.

She's tired and hungry because she forgot to eat lunch again, but it's nearly time to pick up Ashley from school so she takes one of her daughter's chocolate-chip granola bars from the kitchen pantry and brings it upstairs to the office. Mostly it's Brian's office, but Tina uses it sometimes too. She sits down on Brian's swivel chair and feels herself relax a bit as she pivots from side to side in a smooth arc.

And in the glow of the family desktop computer screen, Tina is transported back to her cozy cubicle at her desk right next to Donna's. The small plastic plant pot on the bookshelf next to her that contains only dirt now becomes the large ceramic pot that lovingly held the fat, waxy leaves of the giant jade plant that greeted Tina every morning when she sat down and reached for her mouse on its bright yellow smiley-face pad.

Donna was always there first and she'd say the same two words to Tina when she arrived: "Hello, stranger!"

Which was hilarious because they hadn't been strangers for years, not since Tina's first day, when she was just newly married to Brian and so hopeful about everything.

That day, Katie P. had shown Tina to her desk and trilled, "Here you go! You'll be sitting here, next to Donna! Hi, Donna! This is Tina!"

"Great!" Donna offered their manager a tight smile and gave Tina a brief wave. "Nice to meet you, Tina."

"Nice to meet you, Donna." Tina nodded at her new co-worker as she sank into her cushioned swivel chair, marvelling at how comfortable it was.

Katie P. stood there for a moment longer, blinking at them with her eyelashes flapping like bats. Above the twin coral circles of blush that looked like clown makeup on her light skin, a few stray specks of mascara lingered. "Donna has the best hair of any of us here," she said in a voice full of intensity. "I love your hair, Donna!"

Donna didn't reply.

Katie P. hurried away then, and the jaunty swish-swishing of her sparkly flats on the carpet was soon replaced by the purposeful clickety-clacking of Donna's fingers on her keyboard.

Tina affixed the sticky note with her login name and password to her own blank screen. Katie P. had written the words in pink ink, and all the dots were hearts.

Donna did have nice hair. It was shiny and curly and luxurious. Tina wondered what products she used. Tina had to use a texturizing lotion, a volumizing powder, and a bodifying hairspray just to give her own limp, fine hair the very slightest lift.

The grey fabric of Donna's cubicle panels was brightened by colourful child's drawings of flowers and animals ("To Mommy Love Simone") and her desk was filled with a cheerful assortment of objects, including a snow globe, a tape dispenser shaped like a flamingo, and a pen-and-pencil holder shaped like a cactus. And a framed photograph of herself and a kind-eyed man hugging a gleeful little girl, their three sets of brown arms entwined so tightly it was nearly impossible to tell whose arms were whose.

Tina sighed, and Donna caught her staring.

She reddened. "I've always wanted a snow globe," she said quickly.

"Then you should get yourself one." Donna lifted hers and gave it a shake. "This silly thing always cheers me up."

Tina watched the artificial snow swirling around the miniature skyscrapers. It drifted down and collected at the bottom, burying the minuscule cars on their ribbon of road. "Someday, I hope."

Donna brought the little glass sphere closer to her face and peered in. "I like to pretend I'm a mythical goddess who holds the fates of these teeny-tiny people in their teeny-tiny city in my giant hand," she said. "Will I be merciful? Will I be merciless? Who knows?" She shrugged and replaced the snow globe on her desk. "Depends on the day."

Tina laughed, and Donna grinned at her.

"Let me know if you ever need any help," she said. "I've been here for a while."

"Thanks," said Tina. "I will."

And suddenly the air between and around them was shimmering with possibility.

Tina reaches for the mouse now and clicks on the browser. Her fingers float over the keyboard for a long moment before they descend to type the name "Donna" into the search bar. She wonders why she's never thought of doing this before.

She presses the Enter key and leans forward.

The meaning of "Donna" is "lady."

Tina frowns. She was expecting something better than that.

She carefully creases her granola-bar wrapper to ensure that no sticky crumbs or smears of chocolate end up on the desk, then looks up the name "Simone" next.

It means "to hear or listen."

She nods. That's a good one.

Her own name means "river," but she's pretty sure her mother just chose it because she liked it.

Tina's eyes are getting sore, so she looks away from the screen and watches the snow continue to fall outside. The ground and the trees and her neighbours' roofs are all frosted over. She thinks of gingerbread, and sharp and precarious icicles. If she decided to open up the window and scream right now, the snow would swallow most of the noise.

She hopes the weather will be better for the march tomorrow. But if she's being honest with herself, she and Ashley were never going, anyway.

The snow globe was an impulsive purchase, and Tina regretted it later. But it always cheered her up when she shook it. It reminded her of being young and carefree and running away from a ferocious, barking dog with her friends, and how they were so lucky because they always got away. It reminded her of Donna, who'd said, "Good for you!" when Tina told her she'd gone ahead and ordered it, even though it had been a long time since she'd first expressed interest in Donna's. And she found out she was pregnant not long after the snow globe arrived, so it reminded her of that too.

Then it was in Brian's hand last year, the tiny red sled on the tiny white hill disappearing under an avalanche of plastic particles. And then it was flying, colliding with the TV screen where, just moments before, an army of furious women who looked a lot like Tina but who were so much braver had been marching and chanting with their protest signs held high, and their daughters at their sides.

"Look at them," Ashley had breathed. Her small face was radiant and her eyes were clear, and Tina knew then with absolute certainty that she would be even more amazing than Ashley From High School, who wasn't really that amazing to begin with.

Then Brian said, "This is ridiculous."

Tina checks the clock. She has to leave for the school now. She's only been late picking up Ashley once before, and she'll never do that again. "Where were you?" Ashley had asked with tears on her cheeks when Tina skidded into the office, where her daughter had been waiting alone on a big chair. And Tina had no good answer to give her.

She stands up and hurtles down the stairs and throws on her coat and hat and scarf and jams on her boots, then grabs her house keys from the hall table and yanks open the front door. She's out of time, so she'll have to run.

The snowflakes are everywhere, and she braces herself against the cold as she steps outside and ice crunches under her feet. But she's still carrying some warmth with her, and once she locks the door behind her and starts moving, it's not nearly as bad as she thought it would be.

She picks up speed on the slippery sidewalk, pressing ahead with cautious but determined strides. At the end of their street, she turns and keeps going. All of her is closed against the biting wind, but suddenly she opens her mouth wide. And when the snow rushes in, she starts to sing.

It's a song she remembers because Donna used to sing it a lot, softly but clearly. Tina never asked her the singer's name, and she wishes she had. The song is about feeling good and connecting with the birds and the sun and the fish and the trees.

The words come to her and she lets them out in a strong, loud voice that keeps on getting louder. And she doesn't even care if anyone hears.

PIONEERS

I DO NOT FEEL AT EASE IN THE WOODS. How can anyone feel at ease in the woods?

I don't mind nature. That's not the problem. Nature is fine. I feel at ease surrounded by nature in the city. I feel at ease in parks. I like flowers and trees and birds and squirrels. I do not like sleeping on the ground with only a thin layer of canvas between me and the elements.

But here we are.

Because we had no other choice. Because we couldn't get a cottage because of COVID.

It wasn't for lack of trying. Carl was scouring CottageRental.com non-stop, but because everything was so uncertain and nobody knew what was going to happen, the bookings didn't open up until much later than usual. And even then he couldn't find anything. Which was when he said to me, do you want to try camping this summer?

I wasn't thrilled by the idea, but we had nothing else going on, and I figured, how bad could it be?

Skyler was not impressed when we broke the news about not getting the cottage. She said what was she going to do for five days without the Internet and her YouTubers?

And Carl said to her, "It'll be fun! We can pretend we're pioneers!"

She sniffled and said she didn't know what that was, and he got all excited because Carl loves to talk about history. It's his thing. He got that glint in his eye that he gets whenever history comes up in the conversation, and he explained that pioneers were the olden-days people who discovered Canada and that's why we have Thanksgiving. Those olden-days people are also called *ancestors*, he told Skyler, which is another word for really old people in our family, and every October we say thank you to them for all the farming they did for us.

Skyler wiped a long string of mucus from her nose and said her teacher told her there were people who lived here before the Europeans came and took their land away, and what about them? Were they pioneers too?

Carl blinked at her in slow motion. It was funny to see. Once, twice, three times. Then he looked at me. "They're teaching them that in the first grade now?"

I handed Skyler a Kleenex. "I guess so."

His brow was furrowed. "I would've thought they'd mention that in the principal's newsletter or the parent council newsletter to see how we felt about it first."

I shrugged. "I never read any updates about it."

"I think you should have a word with the principal after we get back." He paused to pick something out of his teeth. "Make sure you say they can talk about all the good stuff. We support all that."

I nodded. "Of course we do."

"Just hold off on the rest of it."

"I'll send her an email," I said, and I made a note on the to-do list on my phone or else I knew it would fly right out of my head. Nothing stays in there anymore, which is unsettling.

Carl went to Costco and purchased all the gear. He asked his friend Todd for some tips, since Todd is a big camper, and Todd told him we needed to keep all our food in a tree at night and we should make sure to bring a shovel to dig a hole to relieve ourselves in. Carl said it's not that kind of camping, and Todd said okay, well bring lots of beer then.

Carl was able to find us a campsite online, but just barely, because so many other people had the same idea. I guess we're lucky. But I don't feel lucky.

I hate camping. It's awful. It's dirty and unpleasant and there is no shower. There is no dock. There is a beach nearby but it's crowded. Nobody is social distancing and they say you're safe if you're outside but I'm just not comfortable sharing my personal space with so many strangers. They play loud, thumping music with offensive lyrics and they splash each other and everyone around them and it's difficult to concentrate on my magazine.

I know I shouldn't complain because I have so many advantages. I should be making better use of my considerable resources and helping in the world more. I should be doing more to make the world a better place, and there are so many people who are doing so much of that good work, and I'm not doing any of it.

The other day I had a voice mail on my phone from a local charity. I listened to it and then I deleted it. They wanted me to call them back, but I didn't want to call them back. They said they had called to thank me for my interest in their organization, but I couldn't remember being interested in their organization and I couldn't figure out how they got my number. Maybe I signed a petition? I sign a lot of petitions and I'm glad I can contribute in that way. I'd rather do things like that, and then they're done. I'm not prepared to do things that are ongoing. I'm not fond of being on committees.

I'm very grateful for what we have and I often tell Skyler she should be grateful as well because so many people have so much less. But then again, all our experiences are subjective, and there are things I am unhappy about too and I'm entitled to that.

I wish our daughter was not so obsessed with video games, for instance. She plays them constantly. It's unhealthy. At least she's getting some sun here. She was starting to look anemic from spending so much time inside with all her devices.

Skyler's on her Switch right now. Because she would rather play video games than sit and gaze at this fire that her mother and father worked so hard to build for her. And we didn't even argue very much! We worked seamlessly as a team, and I was only briefly annoyed at Carl when he gave me some unsolicited advice about twisting the newspaper pages into log shapes. Because I knew that already. Because I'm usually the one who builds the fire at the cottages we rent every summer.

I enjoy the process of collecting the kindling. I find it meditative. Carl said I should get Skyler to pitch in and find some marshmallow sticks, at least, but I knew that would be more trouble than it was worth. Besides, I needed the alone time. He said we should be taking the opportunity to teach her some responsibility for a change. I said if he was so concerned, he could get her to blow up one of the air mattresses. He said but her lungs aren't mature enough. I said fine, just let her keep playing *Animal Crossing* then.

I prefer the log cabin technique to the teepee technique. It just works better for me. It also evokes cheerful memories from my childhood, of crafting log cabins out of Popsicle sticks and glue. The other technique reminds me of how much I wanted to love the little yellow plastic teepee I owned as a child, but it always disappointed me. The day my parents bought it, they set it up for me in the backyard, and I crawled inside immediately and sat cross-legged and imagined I was Tiger Lily from *Peter Pan*. I thought she was so pretty and brave. I dressed up as her once for Halloween when I was about the age Skyler is now. I used to wonder if her character was based on a real person, and every so often I think about googling it. But then I don't. Life is busy.

My little plastic teepee was unbearably hot and stuffy, though, and I began sweating profusely and had to scurry out, gasping for fresh air. Even when we moved it into the shade, that small plastic cone sucked in every single degree of the summer heat and held on to it fiercely. I could never stand to be within its confines for longer than a few minutes. Ultimately we had to throw it away.

Also, the one time I tried making a fire with the teepee technique, the whole thing fell apart and collapsed in on itself. It was very disheartening and I couldn't be bothered to figure out what I was doing wrong. Now I use the log cabin technique exclusively.

I relish the moment when I insert the scrunched-up pieces of newspaper into the spaces between the wooden structure I've constructed and set them all ablaze with the barbecue lighter we brought to make things easier. It's very satisfying. I do sometimes have trouble keeping it going once it's been lit, though. I will acknowledge that occasionally I do need assistance with that part.

In any case, our team effort has produced an excellent fire. Yet all of our daughter's attention is focused on the device in her lap that she's clicking away on. There will be an expression of intense concentration on her small face for a long time, and then she'll look up at us for the briefest moment and proudly proclaim something nonsensical like, "I'm custom-designing a quilt for Tutu because she's cold!"

"Good for you, honey," Carl will say, and I'll roll my eyes, and Skyler will catch me and frown and look away from us again.

Does she even feel the warmth of the real-life fire directly in front of her? Does she even appreciate the work and care that went into creating it? No, she does not. Oh, she'll eat a marshmallow if her mother roasts one for her. But now her mother isn't so sure she wants to.

I am also distracted and preoccupied because my hair is not doing what it's supposed to do. Not just because we're camping and there is no shower and no electricity. Before we left, Carl said I should bring my hair dryer and I could just plug it into the cigarette lighter in the car every morning. I said that's ridiculous.

Now I regret not bringing it.

I haven't visited my hairdresser in so long and now my hair isn't sitting right on my head. My hairline feels higher up than it used to. But maybe it was always that high and I just never noticed? I've started worrying that it might be receding. This possibility is upsetting, and worrying about it saps my energy. If my hair looked better, I could be a better person. I would feel more positive and would have more positive energy to offer to various important causes. I would be more attuned to incidents of injustice in society if I wasn't so focused on whether or not more of my forehead is showing now or if it's just my imagination.

It might be because of my iron levels. I tried to give blood last month because it was something I'd been meaning to do for a long time. I was proud of myself for finally doing it. And during a pandemic too! But when the nurse did the prick test, she told me my iron was too low and I'd have to come back another day when my levels were higher. She gave me a Band-Aid for my finger and I asked if I could take one of the snack-sized bags of Cheetos home for my daughter. She said sorry, those are for donors only, but I snuck one on the way out and put it in my purse when nobody was watching. I'd come all that way, and my intentions were good, and they had been thwarted through no fault of my own.

I'm making more of an effort to eat iron-rich foods after reading on the Internet that low iron levels can lead to receding hairlines in women. I've been taking an iron supplement for a few weeks now and I think I can detect a very subtle difference. I would be so embarrassed if anyone ever saw my search history. I need to remember to erase it.

Why isn't my child more interested in nature? Why does she love screens so much? If we were doing the kind of camping Todd wants us to do, it would not be possible to charge Skyler's device with the car battery every morning and she would be out of luck. But of course I would be enjoying myself even less if we were in a more remote location, and if Skyler was expecting us to entertain her all the time.

But I do like this fire, and it bothers me that Skyler does not appreciate it at all. What is it about video games that she finds so alluring? I would rather sit here in my camping chair with my beer and my hot dog and watch everything burn. The flames are so pretty. I can pick out all sorts of shapes in them. I can listen to the popping and the hissing and imagine there are snakes in there.

Earlier today, I sat on the beach with a decent thriller and a nice Chardonnay in my travel mug. I watched my family frolic in the lake. And I felt at peace. It wasn't as good as the peace I'd be feeling if I were sitting at the end of a dock on a Muskoka chair with a frosty margarita on the armrest and the reflections of majestic pine trees surrounding me in a semicircular formation. But it still felt good.

And I felt badly about that.

I know there is so much suffering in the world, and I know that I am fortunate to feel those peaceful feelings. But should I feel guilty for feeling them? Because those feelings arose out of love, and why should I feel guilty about that?

I love my family. I love our fully detached Edwardian-style house. We're currently in the process of renovating because there's not quite enough room for me and Carl to both work from home comfortably. We're adding one more floor so we can have our offices on the second and third floors, and Skyler and the nanny can have the entire main floor and the basement to themselves, to do whatever it is they do while Carl and I are doing our work.

My point is, I know that everyone just wants the freedom to love their families and their homes without being worried. That's something we all have in common. Also, there is peace and there is tranquility.

I am definitely not tranquil here.

I wasn't sleeping well before this trip and now I can't sleep at all. How can I?

We parked the car really close to the tent, and I keep the keys right next to me in a Tupperware container in case a bear attacks in the middle of the night and we need to unbeep the car. Carl says we should just keep the doors unlocked, but I said what about thieves, and he said okay fine have it your way.

So yes, the safety of the car is accessible to us. But how exactly would we manoeuvre there safely with a giant marauding bear in our path? Before we left, I read about the best ways to deal with a bear if one were to appear, but I know I will forget all of it if I'm ever actually put to the test.

And guess what? There is a bear in the area. There was a sign that said so on our way in. When Carl told Todd about the spot we'd booked, Todd said, "Oh yeah, it's nice there. But just so you know, you might see a sign when you drive in that says, 'Bear in Area.' But don't freak out because that sign is always there."

"Okay," I said, when Carl told me that later. "Okay."

It was the night before we were leaving and we were in bed. My heart started beating faster and that was frustrating because it meant it would take me even longer to fall asleep. I was going to have to take a lot of deep breaths to calm myself down and relax my body enough to finally drift off.

"Plus," said Carl, "Todd said we would definitely hear it coming."

"What?"

"Todd said if there's a bear in the woods near our tent at night, it will sound like a freight train. So as soon as we hear that, we just get out of the tent and run to the car, no problem."

"Right," I said. "Good to know."

The first night in the tent, I didn't fall asleep until dawn. I lay there listening to the crackling of dry leaves and the hooting of owls and an unidentifiable rustling that would start and stop and start again. I only felt safe enough to close my eyes when the first weak rays of sunlight made my sleeping husband and daughter visible to me, when they had previously been invisible.

In the middle of the second night, I cried. I tried to be quiet so I wouldn't wake up Skyler, but then I started full-on weeping. I confessed to Carl that I was terrified of the imminent trip to the outhouse I was going to have to take. I had consumed two tall cans of a strong IPA after seven o'clock, which was a bad idea, and I know that now, but here I am doing it again, and I did it last night too because it makes me feel better.

Carl told me to be quiet and just pee by the car, but I'd read on an outdoorsman's blog that bears are attracted to the smell of human urine so I didn't want my pee to be so close to our tent. Eventually I worked up the courage to grab a flashlight and put on my flip-flops, and I loudly hummed a tune all the way to the outhouse, because I read that if you make a lot of noise when you're walking through the forest, you won't accidentally surprise a bear. The outhouse wasn't far away but it felt far. The older man at the campsite beside ours shouted at me to shut up, but I ignored him and kept humming.

I will not be ashamed of my fear of nature. I have survived this long, and now we only have one more night to go, thank God, and this beer is making me feel better.

And Skyler is having fun. This morning she woke up rested and revitalized after sleeping serenely through the entire endless night, and she gave me the sweetest smile and said, "Can we do this all the time, Mommy?"

I said haha, that sounds nice. But no. I said maybe we could set up the tent for her in our backyard sometime, would she like that? That seemed to appease her, and she was also excited about being allowed to eat a miniature box of Frosted Flakes for breakfast, so hopefully she won't ask me that again.

There are too many unknowns here. There is too much that is beyond my control and I don't like it. I know that control is only an illusion, but I cling to the notion of it anyway. Especially now.

Last night was the worst. I gave up on the outhouse because it was too far away so I just peed beside the car like Carl suggested. Then of course I was worried that the smell would attract bears so I kicked some dirt over the pee, but some of the pee transferred to at least one of my flip-flops, and I realized I was creating a urine-scented trail leading directly to our tent. Fortunately, there were no repercussions.

I am not sure if I will pee beside the car again tonight. I didn't like the sensation of fear-squatting there, exposed to the elements on all sides with my jogging pants around my ankles, with my bare ass glowing in the moonlight and possibly being visible to the older man in the neighbouring campsite. It wasn't pleasant, but neither was the walk to the outhouse.

Thankfully, tonight will be the final night I am faced with that choice. Starting tomorrow, I will never sleep in a tent again in my life, unless I have to.

And when would I ever have to? The end of the world? COVID feels like that sometimes. I miss doing all the things I used to do. I miss our cottage vacations and European vacations and all-inclusive resort vacations and movie theatres and parties. I want things to go back to normal. But I know there are families fleeing war and famine right at this minute, living in refugee camps and sleeping in tents because they have no other options. When that thought occurred to me earlier today, I decided to give an extra donation to the Red Cross as soon as we got home. Or at least immediately after we unpacked.

I know that I'm lucky. But I don't think I need to feel bad about it.

Carl's wiener falls off his stick onto the coals, and he swears. "Should've brought the fondue forks," he grumbles, and I'm waiting for Skyler to tell him he said a bad word but she's too busy selecting a new outfit for her character.

"You can't just leave it in there," I tell him.

"Why not?"

I lean closer to him with raised eyebrows. "Animals," I whisper.

I glance over at Skyler but she's not paying attention. Her character looks sort of like her but sort of not like her. The hair is shorter. I wonder if that means anything.

"I can't just reach in there and pull it out," says Carl. "It's hot."

"Fine. Just remember to throw it away later."

"Okay," he says, "but you have to remind me."

A mosquito buzzes near my ear and I smack it dead between my hands. "Fine." I take another drink. I am going to have three cans tonight and I don't even care.

"Mommy, can I have a marshmallow?" Skyler asks without looking up. "Can you cook it for me?"

"Who said that?" I say, pretending to be startled off my chair.

Skyler doesn't laugh.

"Don't they have marshmallows in that magical land you're so fascinated by?" I ask her. "Can't one of your village people roast one for you?"

"It's not magical, Mommy. And they're not people. They're called *villagers*." At last she wrenches her eyes away from the device and gives me a look I can't decipher. She seems like a child from another planet sometimes. "Please can I have one?"

"Of course you can." I have the urge to hug her but I stab a marshmallow for her instead and thrust it into the fire. "Thank you for saying 'please.'"

She smiles at me before she goes back to her game, and for a moment I am brimming with good feelings. My whole body is overflowing with them like a cornucopia spilling out apples and pears and pumpkins and corn. Then that moment passes.

Last night, after I peed by the car and then frantically hurled my flip-flops into the woods, I crawled into our tent and zipped up the flap and encased myself in my damp sleeping bag. I felt every single rock and twig through my flimsy air mattress, and I tried to get cozy, but it didn't work. Every tiny noise outside was amplified. I was one hundred per cent convinced that at any second I was going to hear a freight train crashing and bellowing through the trees and bushes. My heart was hammering in my chest and I was basically panting when I told Carl, in a hushed and shaky voice that was nonetheless filled with resolve, that I would never, ever go camping again as long as I lived. He mumbled something unintelligible and rolled over.

After that, I checked my phone frequently, counting down the minutes until dawn. Or at least until the time right before dawn, when the total and complete darkness would relent and the dim, soothing silhouettes would begin to materialize—my hand in front of my face, the Tupperware container with our car keys in it, the slumbering forms of my husband and daughter beside me.

How did they sleep so soundly every single night? How was that possible?

I lay there and waited to be reassured that soon enough, like always, the light would eventually return.

MOMENTS WITH MUSTAFA

EVERY TIME I SEE THE LIBRARY SECURITY GUARD, I ask him something new about himself. We are getting to know each other, and the process has been such a rich and rewarding experience.

His name is Mustafa, which I didn't have to ask about because he wears a name tag, so the first time we met last week, I said to him, "Hello, Mustafa. I'm Darlene. I live in the neighbourhood and I bet you have roots in the Middle East, don't you?" I know it's not polite these days to ask where someone is from, so what I like to do is turn it into a fun guessing game.

He didn't answer that particular query with words, but his warm brown eyes twinkled at me over his face mask, which I took to mean yes. And then another time I overheard him talking to one of the librarians about Kandahar, which I googled when I got home (and luckily the search bar knew how to spell it because I sure didn't!) and, woohoo, I guessed right!

I'm very grateful for this opportunity to connect with someone who is different from me. But of course not so different after all! Because we are both human beings with hopes and dreams and worries and families and favourite foods. I told Mustafa how much I enjoy falafels and dates and basically anything with coconut in it, and sometimes the occasional shawarma wrap when I'm feeling a bit wild. But no garlic sauce, please! It repeats on me. I asked him if he's ever tried schnitzel and he shook his head, probably because he didn't know what it was, and I said if he ever wants to sample the cuisine of *my* people, he should hop on the 401 and grab a table at the Edelweiss Tavern in Kitchener, pronto. They also serve the best boneless wings there. Of course, he'll have to wait until the restrictions are lifted. In the meantime, I told him with a wink, I make a killer Fleischsalat!

One day I said to Mustafa, "I bet you trained for a better career in your home country, didn't you?" Because too often this seems to be the case with new Canadians and that's not fair, so it's important for us to recognize their unsung accomplishments and their unrealized goals. Mustafa has his own unique and special story, and yet most people never even bother to ask him about it. For instance, there are often other library patrons in line to pick up their holds and not once have I ever seen any of them asking Mustafa anything. No, I take that back—once an elderly man asked him when the library was closing. Isn't that awful?

Whereas I have gleaned from my diligent and persistent inquiries that Mustafa has a six-year-old daughter and a ten-year-old son and a wife who is a front-line worker at a factory although I can't remember what they do there. But the bottom line is that it's hard work and I said to him one day, "Mustafa, it's shameful how we treat our front-line workers. They're the real heroes and we call them heroes but we definitely don't treat them like heroes, do we?" And he shook his head sadly, and I shook my head sadly too, and then it started to rain so I had to get going.

Mustafa's skin is the colour of a copper penny—that useful and helpful coin that Canada has callously discarded in the name of "progress." But I still keep a big jar of pennies on my bookshelf at home, and once in a while I empty them all out onto my bed so I can admire them. I appreciate them for the understated but undeniable beauty they bring to the world.

But others are not so appreciative. I asked Mustafa one morning if he had ever been the victim of racism in this country because people think Canada is so much better than America but we're not. And proving my point exactly, Mustafa said yes. And that was so upsetting. I told Mustafa I felt terrible that happened to him and how the whole rotten situation just makes me feel so helpless, and then I started to cry. I was embarrassed by my outburst but thankfully there was no one else around to see it except for Mustafa, whose brown eyes telegraphed kindness and empathy and concern. I could tell he wanted to comfort me but couldn't because of the rules about physical distancing. The distress was evident in his agitated posture as he glanced left and right, ensuring my privacy until I could compose myself.

That was a really special moment between us. A fusing of the souls happened between me and him and his entire family and all of the other unfortunate recipients of Islamophobia he probably knows, and I slept so peacefully that night. Which was a relief since I haven't been sleeping very well lately because of how close I came to death recently, and so I was extra thankful for my moments with Mustafa because these interactions have helped to put things in perspective for me.

Yes I had a biopsy and yes that was incredibly stressful but it turned out to be negative so I don't have breast cancer even though I easily could have. But none of that matters in the big scheme of things, and I've learned that valuable life lesson from Mustafa, who has a chair but I have never seen him sitting in it even though he could probably use a rest once in a while. His arms and legs are so skinny and he's not very tall. If we were allowed to stand back-to-back, which we're not because we have to stay two metres apart, I bet the top of his head would only come up to my neck, even with his cap on. This does not seem to be an ideal body type for a security guard. But I suppose libraries are generally calm places that attract calm people, so Mustafa is probably not called into service very often.

His chair is made of flimsy plastic and one day I watched as one of the librarians affixed a hand-lettered sign to the chair that read: *SECRITY GUARD*. The spelling mistake annoyed me so much! It felt like a manifestation of how little she cared about him. I didn't notice the error right away but then I did, and then it was impossible to unsee it.

In the same way, I think about how it is impossible to unsee a person's humanity once we have truly glimpsed it. Only then can we look beyond the cardboard-cut-out clichés portrayed by mainstream media, which are so damaging. The stereotypes we've been marinating in since birth like a poisonous brine are clogging the tubes of genuine mutuality, so we must do whatever we can to unclog them.

I will freely admit that I have watched and enjoyed *24* and *Homeland* and *Jack Ryan* and countless other TV shows and films that depict practitioners of the Muslim faith as enemies to be feared, and I used to get anxious around men who looked like the bad men in those shows and films. But Mustafa does not make me anxious. I don't worry about him like some people would. He makes me feel serene. He's here keeping us safe. Along with all the books and the other library materials too. I can also relate to the pain of being demonized by the media because my mother's great-great-great-grandparents were born in Munich, or was it Dresden, and Germans have certainly received their own unfair share of persecution in popular entertainment!

But it is possible (and preferable!) to rid ourselves of those harmful biases—all you need is the will and the inclination to dig beneath the surface and to demonstrate sincere interest in what you find. Mustafa is not a terrorist, as Hollywood would have us believe. He is a sweet and loving and totally benign father of two with a wife who works in a factory and she almost died from COVID twice but she didn't and thank God for that.

Mustafa told me that the library staff were all very accommodating when he needed to take time off when his wife was ill. I asked if he got paid for that time off and he said no. He said it quietly because he was probably worried about being fired if he complained too loudly or publicly about his working conditions.

I told him that I have personally written letters to our premier and the minister of labour to demand paid sick days for every worker and that I will continue to do so, and I don't mind doing it at all. I could tell from the thoughtful way he creased his brow that he was thankful, which made me feel good.

Meanwhile, when I told my friend Janine about my letters, she said when did you turn into an activist all of a sudden? And I said it's our responsibility as people with privilege to use our power to fight the good fight. She said okay whatever, and I didn't push the discussion any further because I know that political conversations can make some people uncomfortable.

I also told Janine that I have been talking to Mustafa and she said he should be grateful because our troops are over there keeping his family safe. In order to challenge her skewed preconceptions (but gently, so she wouldn't get offended), I pointed out that his family lives here, in Canada. She said well he's probably got a grandmother or grandfather over there, at least. I said yes maybe, but he hasn't told me about them yet.

One day I brought Mustafa some Timbits. I got him an assortment including chocolate and sour-cream glazed and the birthday-cake kind with sprinkles and the apple-fritter ones my son used to love when he was little but suddenly he's off gluten so who knows anymore. Anyway, he's off at university now so he can eat what he wants, I don't care. All of his classes are online and he still moved away but it's his life and I hope he's happy with it. I slid the box underneath

Mustafa's chair and instructed him in a playfully stern voice, "Don't you dare share those with anybody!"

He said thank you in the nicest, softest way but he didn't reach for the box, so he must have excellent willpower because I would've opened it immediately and gobbled up at least two right off the bat, starting with the chocolate ones. Then I supposed he was probably holding off because he was wearing the face mask, so maybe he'd eat them on his break.

After I met Mustafa, I read a reference book about the Arab world and its inhabitants, which made me feel more informed. Because it's crucial to enrich our knowledge and understanding of each other so we can bridge the deep divides between us. Before I read the book, in my mind Mustafa's home country looked like a mishmash of the faraway and exotic lands from the *Indiana Jones* movies (which I loved, but what I *didn't* love was the very unfair and hurtful implication in *Raiders of the Lost Ark* that all Germans were Nazis like the creepy villain whose face melts off at the end). It still sort of looks like that in my head, but a more factual version. Non-fiction doesn't really captivate me, though, so now I'm back to thrillers.

It's vital that we keep learning, however, and it's our responsibility to educate ourselves. It's no longer acceptable to simply smile and wave at unfamiliar members of our population and then continue on our merry way. We need to stop and ask them questions about themselves and pay close attention to their answers. We need to let them know that we're on a marvellous voyage of discovery, and what we want to discover is...everything about them! The day I took home that reference book, I showed Mustafa the cover with its glossy photo montage of sand dunes and palm trees and the pyramids and a mosque with pointy towers that looked like the Sultan's Palace from *Aladdin*, and he nodded in a solemn but friendly way. I won't lie—that made me feel pretty good.

I feel sorry for the other library patrons who never even bother to say a word to this wonderful man who has brought me so much fulfilment. Some of them don't even acknowledge his presence! Like he's a statue standing there. Like he's not even a fellow human being with thoughts and feelings and desires. They stare at their phones and when it's their turn to go in, they just pick up their holds and then they sanitize their hands and their minds and walk away. As if Mustafa wasn't even there. I do occasionally see someone saying hello to him, but they think that's enough.

But I'm going much further than that, with gusto and enthusiasm. Because I care. Because Mustafa matters to me. His beating heart under his navy-blue security-guard jacket matters to me. I can feel it thumping inside my own rib cage, hard and fluttery and insistent.

My heart was beating so fast when I was inside the MRI machine, but I couldn't move. I had to lie completely still. Nestled in one loose fist was the ball I could squeeze if panic overcame me, my hand enveloping it so lightly that I barely felt it at all. But its presence was soothing all the same, and I imagined I was lying on a beach with a gentle breeze blowing through my hair. That stream of air was in fact being generated by a fan somewhere far inside the tunnel to keep me as cool and comfortable as possible in my stretched-out and prone position, motionless and face down with my left breast fitted into a hole and held there, waiting for another part of the machine to whir to life and slice into me.

I felt the smooth sand of the imaginary beach beneath me and there was a boat in the water and the *blam-blam-blam* of the MRI machine was an alarm because something was wrong and now all the passengers were jumping off the sides, falling into the ocean with dramatic splashes and who knows what happened to them then. They weren't wearing life-jackets, so most of them probably drowned. Or else sharks came and ate them.

I wonder if Mustafa and his family experienced something like that when they made their long and arduous journey to Canada. Did they come over on a boat? I haven't asked him that yet but I will. It's impossible to fathom the horrors that refugees have to endure just to find safety and security here. (And now Mustafa is bringing safety and security to others! Perhaps that's what drew him to this job.) And then they have to contend with racists on top of that. The inequity and prejudice that Mustafa faces on a daily basis are real, and I accept his lived reality and honour it by acknowledging the barriers that exist for him but not for me.

I also know what it's like to worry about the future. There was a long period of many days before I got the test results when my destiny was forked into two paths, and it could have gone either way. Both directions were equally possible, and unlived moments from both of those futures would flash at me constantly. I was doing a lot of online shopping during that time, and I bought a new pair of fleece pyjamas with a snowflake pattern that I loved. But then I envisioned myself wearing them and having breast cancer, which at a certain point felt inevitable. My legs inside the plushy fabric would be swollen from edema, which I learned can be a side effect of chemotherapy. I imagined the snowflakes swirling around my bloated legs and that image was unrelenting, so I donated the pyjamas to Value Village, and my husband said well that was another unnecessary purchase, wasn't it? Which was so insensitive I wanted to scream.

I asked Mustafa, "Were there security guards at the library before COVID?" Because I can't remember ever seeing a library security guard before the pandemic, and I used to go to the library a lot. That's why I come here so often now. I can't stay away! I miss browsing, though. I miss meandering up and down the aisles and gazing at the multicoloured spines arranged on the shelves, each one promising something fresh and new. I miss picking out a book at random and reading what it's about and then most of the time I would just put it back because I'm very particular with my likes and dislikes. But I love books in general and I love to read. I love the escapism.

I usually go for thrillers, as I mentioned, because my life isn't very exciting. I had my son young, so now I'm an empty-nester at fifty, and my husband and I don't have much to talk about anymore. The other day, I had something I really wanted to tell him but then I forgot what it was, so we just sat there on the couch watching TV and not saying anything to each other like usual. Then I remembered the thing! But then I said it, and it turned out that what I wanted to tell him was that I'd been investigating online if sand can go in the green bin, because sometimes I shake sand out of my shoes into the green bin but maybe that isn't the right thing to do. And in the process I found out that due to COVID we're not supposed to put Kleenex or paper towels in the green bin anymore. Because of germs, I guess. But how were we supposed to know that? It's not like they're publicizing it or anything! I've been putting Kleenex and paper towels in our green bin all along! And then I was so horrified that *this* was the thing I was so excited to tell my husband. So then we were quiet again.

I prefer the kind of story that keeps you on the edge of your seat wondering what's going to happen next. The last one I read was about a man who tricks a woman into marrying him by being charming and then he locks her up in a room. *Ooh*, I thought when that happened, but it turned out he didn't want to have sex with her, which would've been something. Instead he just wanted to torment and torture her in a non-sexual way, which was a letdown. Maybe I'm developing a tolerance and I need my thrillers to be more and more thrilling to keep me invested in the story. We'll see.

Anyway, something weird happened yesterday and I'm still trying to figure it out. I arrived at the library and got in line and there was Mustafa and I waved at him, but he didn't wave back. Instead he turned around and went inside. He was moving quickly, as if he'd forgotten something.

And then a librarian walked out, the one who gave me a hard time last month for forgetting my library card at home and I said but can't you just type my name into your system? And she said yes but she clearly wasn't happy about that. She came outside and stood by Mustafa's chair with her arms crossed, and when I was at the top of the ramp standing on the yellow X in front of the door, she said to me in an unkind voice, "Mustafa needs a break."

"Okay," I said, and I nodded because that was a good thing. Of course he should get a break instead of standing there in the hot sun all day. Yesterday was a scorcher and the summer hasn't even started yet.

"You can go in," she told me. "There's nobody else ahead of you."

So I thanked her and went in and said hello to the nicer librarian who was sitting behind the table. She reminds me of my favourite aunt on my dad's side, even though she's probably about the same age as I am. She's patient like Aunt Kathy was, and she might even be Scottish too. I placed my card on the tray, and she smiled and carried the tray over to the computer and then went to the shelf and found my hold. She scanned it in and brought me my book and slid the tray back along the table to return my card.

The whole time I was looking around for Mustafa, but he wasn't anywhere to be seen. Was he over in the periodicals area? No. Was he over in the children's section? No. Maybe he was in the washroom?

"There's someone waiting," the nice librarian said to me in her compassionate voice, and I thought of Aunt Kathy's hugs that always smelled like the scones or shortbread she liked to bake, and how her soft arms would wrap around me and she'd call me the sausage in her sausage roll.

"You have a good day now," the nice librarian said benevolently, and I thanked her and made my exit so the next person could come in.

The mean librarian was standing outside frowning at me and I didn't want to talk to her but Mustafa still hadn't returned to his post so I asked her, "Is Mustafa okay? Is he sick?"

She shrugged. "You could say that."

"Oh no," I said. "Will you please give him my best?"

She said sure, but in a hostile and begrudging way. Like maybe she would but maybe she wouldn't, and I'd never be the wiser. About a year ago, I asked her where she was from and she said Barrie, and that wasn't the answer I'd been expecting so I figured she was being difficult on purpose. I guess that's just her personality. It's sad when people are so closed off like that.

So I left. I walked down the ramp and kept going, but when I turned the corner around the building to start heading home, I heard the front door open. I stopped and peeked around the corner, and there was Mustafa.

He looked just fine to me. He didn't look sick at all. Then the mean librarian gave him the thumbs-up for some reason, and he went back to standing in his spot and she went back inside.

Something about the exchange didn't sit right with me and I almost went back to ask him about it, but suddenly I didn't have the energy. The heat was making me droopy and tired, and all I wanted to do was go home and lie on the couch in the air conditioning with a big bowl of ice cream and my new thriller.

I closed my eyes, and my fingers went to the hard lump that has formed at the biopsy site, which I know is just a hematoma. I looked it up on the Internet and my family doctor reassured me too. It's just a harmless, normal thing. A collection of blood under the skin, that's all. At first it was the size of a plum but now it's only the size of a cherry. It's shrinking. It will eventually go away and not be there anymore.

Somebody at the breast clinic or the MRI clinic should've told me, though. Or the possibility should've been included in the aftercare pamphlet the nurse gave me before he inserted the IV for the contrast dye. Before he did that, I had been soothed by his gentle manner and I wondered about his background. But after his skillful caramel-hued hands slid the needle into my arm, I couldn't think of anything except what the test might find, and the whole room went blurry and white, and then the nice man's mouth was moving but I heard absolutely nothing at all.

All along, a helpful bullet point might have said, *the worst possible thing you have been told that you could ever find in your breast is a hard lump, but after you have the MRI-guided biopsy to determine whether or not you have breast cancer, you might find a hard lump in your breast but DON'T WORRY! This is not the bad kind of lump! This is only your body's reaction to the trauma of the needle going in and cutting out samples of your tissue from the suspicious area! There is absolutely no need to panic about this particular lump!*

I know there's no need to panic. The ordeal is over and I got through it and then I did a good thing.

I'm not going to get all hysterical like the wife I'm reading about now, who finds out that her husband has another family in another town, so she kills him and starts stalking the other wife and her kids. But then the tables turn and she becomes paranoid that someone is trying to kill *her*! Probably the other wife, who are we kidding. Of course it's her, who else would it be?

It's not bad so far, though. I'm starting to get excited about how it will end, which is an encouraging sign.

OUT FOR A WALK

YOU ARE OUT FOR A WALK and up ahead there is a construction site. A house has been draped in sheets of cloudy plastic with ladders and scaffolding pressed up against it. That means there will be people there, and you think about crossing the street, but you don't. You keep walking.

This is a mistake.

You get closer to the house and now you see the workers and now they see you. There are about a dozen of them, all older white men with white beards, and they stop hammering and drilling and whatever else they were doing. Painting? They are wearing white uniforms but none of them are wearing masks.

You forgot your mask at home. You should always have one handy for moments like this. Just put the mask in your pocket and go. You should be doing that every single time. The next time you head out for a walk, that's what you'll do for sure.

It's very quiet. There is only the sound of your shoes on the concrete. But now you can't remember if the workers were making noise before. Construction sites are usually loud places but this silence doesn't feel sudden. It feels like a continuation. But that can't be right.

You keep walking. The day is full of blue sky and the white M-shaped wings of gulls soaring through it. Up until right now, you were enjoying being outside in this lovely weather. It's been cold for so long and now it's warmer, it's almost spring, and you need to get some colour in your face.

You keep waiting for the workers to go back to work but they don't.

You delay being afraid by thinking that you should've brought the library book that is overdue. You need to return it. Other people are waiting for it to become available. But there are no late fees anymore so you keep forgetting. So those people will have to keep waiting, thanks to you.

You're also far away from the library because you're in the neighbourhood where your old house is, where you used to live when you were a child. Before your parents moved to a bigger house in a newer subdivision. That was years ago, and that is where you visit them now with your husband and your daughter. You all sit in their giant backyard on lawn chairs placed at least two metres apart and you know you are lucky they even have a backyard but you're still getting tired of it. You came here today for some nostalgia and because you're also getting tired of walking around the neighbourhood where you live now with your own family, with its parks and laneways and leafy side streets that you're grateful for but bored of.

The house where the construction is happening is familiar, and you think maybe it's the one where you scowled at that lady on her front lawn all those years ago. She was standing right there in front of her red-brick bungalow with her arms crossed, and you passed by with your mom and your aunt, and the woman scowled at you so you scowled back.

No, but this house is not a bungalow. And you were smaller then.

Maybe this is the house where the hunter lived. One day he hung a dead moose by its hind legs on a sturdy branch of the giant maple tree in his front yard and then butchered it there, piece by piece. As the days went on, there was less and less of the moose until it wasn't even recognizable as an animal anymore. It was just a red and purple and brown and white thing that all the kids would crowd around and stare at. A boy touched it once, but he wouldn't tell anyone what it felt like.

No, but there is no tree here. Isn't it funny how memories are.

You wonder who lives here now. You wonder what kind of work these men are doing. You could guess but you'd probably be wrong. You've never been a handy person. You leave all that stuff to your husband.

In the moment when you scowled at the lady on her front lawn, she saw you do it and her eyes narrowed. She had frizzy red hair in a tight ponytail and she was wearing a pink tracksuit. Her arms uncrossed so she could point at you, and she yelled at your mother, "Your kid just made a face at me!"

You were maybe eight years old at the time. This is the age your daughter is now and she knows everything. Not really, but some days you think that. She is gathering information all the time. She is always asking you and your husband what you were like as children. You should tell her the story of that time you scowled at the mean lady on her front lawn. You should tell her the story of the hunter and the moose with no skin. Or is that one too gruesome?

"What kind of face?" your mother wanted to know.

The lady said, "A bad one!"

And you remember feeling powerful then because even though you'd done the thing the lady said you did, you did it for the right reasons. A grown-up had scowled at you and your family and you'd scowled back in self-defence. And you were just a kid, and your mother knew you were a good girl who didn't go around giving bad looks to people who didn't deserve them. You rarely got in trouble, and if you did it was just for fighting with your brother, not anything to do with people you didn't know. All your life you had lived in this neighbourhood, but all this time you'd never noticed this lady before. And then she was standing there with her hands on her hips saying to your mother, "I'm waiting for an apology." And you waited for what your mother would say.

You walk past the workers. Some are up on ladders or scaffolding and some are standing on the bright green grass. They're strangers who are watching you, but there's a sameness about them that's comforting. They could be your dad or your uncle or your dentist.

You like your dentist. He's a good guy and you trust him completely. You've been going to him since you were a kid and now your husband and daughter go to him too. He keeps a treasure box filled with cheap plastic toys that you loved when you were little and your daughter loves now. His moon-white hands are covered with thick, dark hair that pokes through his latex gloves. You used to think he was a werewolf but he's always so gentle when he puts his fingers in your mouth.

The boy who touched the skinned moose used to chase you and your friends around. Once he picked you up and hoisted you onto his shoulder and you were helpless and your butt was sticking up in the air next to his face. You were embarrassed, but something about what he was doing also made you excited. He made a comment about your butt being big and then he put his hand on it. He spread his fingers wide. And then he let you go.

You liked him. But not really. You didn't like him for who he was. You liked him for the dirty way he looked at you and talked about you. Once he came up really close and his face was intense and porpoise-like, his skin stretching across his bulging forehead under his buzzed blond hair and straining against his massive jaw and flashing teeth, and he stared at you hard and said, "Wanna screw?" And you didn't know what he meant but you sort of did. You knew it meant something to do with sex, whatever sex was. And in that moment, on your street with the squares of front lawns, and shade from the trees up and down the road except where you were standing—the sun hot and bright—you almost opened your mouth to say yes. There was nothing else but you and him. And then he opened up the grubby fingers of his closed fist and showed you a small silver object.

You keep walking past the construction site and the tall men. It's way too late to cross the street. At this point you're just trying to put as much distance between you and the workers as possible. This is tricky because they're more spaced out now, less focused on their work and more focused on you. They're climbing down from the scaffolding and climbing down from the ladders. The plastic sheets hanging from the scaffolding are flapping in the ominous wind that has just picked up, and the blue sky is now grey.

By this point you're used to doing the avoidance dance, the way everyone politely agrees in an unspoken way to get out of each other's path because of germs. But the men in white aren't doing that. They're closing in around you. Or maybe that's just your imagination.

Your mom had frowned and glanced between you and the angry neighbour lady. This was an unusual situation and she was surprised. She was trying to figure it out.

It was a beautiful day and you had been enjoying that walk with your mom and your aunt, who was visiting from a different city. Earlier the three of you had gone to see the miniature replica of your town, which used to be something for tourists to do here but then it was torn down so now there's nothing. You loved the little streets and houses and cars and shops and tiny people frozen in various tableaus, including the dramatic scene with the house on fire. That was your favourite part, with all the tiny firefighters in their little red fire truck trying to rescue everyone. The figurines were small and slightly misshapen so the expressions on their faces were hard to discern, but there was undeniable terror in the way the residents of the burning home were posed with their tiny arms reaching out of the little top-floor windows with the flickering orange light inside.

"I'm sure my daughter didn't mean it," said your mom.

"Oh, she meant it," said the lady.

She was so angry, and you were triumphant.

Your mom sighed and looked at you. "Say you're sorry, then."

Your eyes widened. You had not expected this.

And you were about to refuse, to rail against the injustice of this situation, but your mom and your aunt were giving you disappointed looks. So you apologized, and the lady grinned like it was the best day of her stupid life.

The tallest of the men comes closer and smiles and says something to you. Something blandly conversational about today being a nice day, isn't it? And you nod to appease him.

You're surrounded now, but there's a clear path between the construction-site house and the red-brick bungalow beside it. You smile back at the man, just a slight curve of your mouth in acknowledgement but not encouraging any further chit-chat because when people open their mouths to speak, the air fills with the virus and you are not wearing a mask.

You don't like to wear a mask when it's just you and you're out for a walk. You can dodge passersby well enough, ensure there is enough social distance between you and them to stay safe. But the man is coming closer so you swerve onto that path between the houses and quicken your pace, and there are men in white everywhere now, more and more of them. Just you and them and nobody else.

But you grew up on this street so you know there are no fences here. At least, there didn't use to be. The neighbours all liked to pretend that their land was expansive and endless. So if you just keep going, you'll pass through the backyards and reach the next street over and then you can run.

Except there's something in your way.

You stop in front of rolls of white carpet. Long and lumpy, stacked side by side and on top of each other. You didn't notice them before but now they're impossible to miss. There are too many of them to step over, but you might be able to climb.

When you get closer, though, you know they're not really rolls of carpet. They're something else, and the realization makes you stumble sideways and lose your momentum. You turn and hurry away and now you're back on the sidewalk of your old street and the tallest man is following you. You're walking backwards so he can't sneak up on you and he's looking at you intently.

"It's not what you think," he says. "Don't worry." His teeth are large and square and there are sharp white bristles on his pointed chin. He's wearing a white painter's cap and white overalls and this outfit makes him look official, like he knows what he's doing.

The other men go back to work. They climb their ladders and their scaffolding and disappear into the dark holes of the house. They emerge with more rolled-up carpets, which must be heavy because it takes two men to lift each one. They have to co-operate. The men carry their bundles down to the ground and their hard white boots flatten the soft green grass. They drop their loads onto the growing pile and then they go back for more.

Each rolled-up carpet falls onto the others with a dull thud that frightens the small brown birds huddled in the neighbour's hedge. Their wings rustle and whoosh as they all fly up, filling the air with their frantic chirping before they descend and settle back onto the branches again.

"We're not doing anything wrong," the tall man tells you, speaking more quickly now. "We're just working here."

As if you'd scolded him and he's offering an apology.

"You're not wearing a mask," you say. "You should all be wearing masks, but you're not."

"Neither are you," he says, and he opens his arms wide and his smile broadens. "But you're right. We all need to follow the rules."

You're still walking backwards and you know there's a ditch coming up and you're going to fall if you're not careful. This neighbourhood is imprinted on you. You used to walk home from school through these ditches and you'd invent imaginary scenarios like you were an explorer on a jungle adventure, hacking through the underbrush and jumping over quicksand.

Once three older boys found you alone and caught you muttering to yourself and they thought that was funny. They were following too closely and snickering to each other. You knew they wanted to do something bad to you and you could tell they were working up to it, so you ran as fast as you could. And they chased you, and you imagined they were zombies with their black eyes and pasty faces and outstretched arms. But luckily you were almost home, and when you reached your driveway it was as if you'd stepped through a forcefield. You were safe. The boys stood there across the street for a long moment, and then they went away.

You were always safe at home. Your daughter is safe at home now. Sometimes you're even grateful that the pandemic is keeping all of you locked up inside because that means you can keep her close. You should be encouraging her to be independent, she's at the age for that now. She should be ready to walk to school unaccompanied by adults like you did, but there is no school now beyond the screen she sits in front of, so you can relax. You can keep her close for a while longer and nobody will judge you.

"Yep, sure is a nice day to be out for a walk," says the tall man. "Do you live around here?"

"No." You'd almost forgotten he was there. "Not anymore."

"Yeah." He winks as if you're in on a joke together. "It's gone a bit downhill, hasn't it?"

He's friendlier than you'd expected. He's not chasing you. He just wants to explain.

Your heartbeat slows and you start thinking about what you'll make for dinner tonight. You've really been embracing cooking lately. It boosts your mood. It's always a challenge to find meals that all three of you will enjoy, but it's a fun challenge.

The tall man tips his cap at you in a courteous way. "You take care now."

Then he rejoins the other men at the house and goes back to doing whatever it is they're doing. Just working. That's all.

It really is a nice day. The wind is only a gentle breeze now and the sky is blue again. It's good to take these daily strolls. It's vital for your mental health. To be out in nature, or what counts for nature in the city, and have some time to yourself and feel the sun on your cheeks before you head back home.

Your phone buzzes and it's your husband with a text that makes you blush. You're warm and happy and you decide this wasn't the street you grew up on after all. And even if it was, you don't recognize it anymore. It has nothing to do with you or anyone you know. It's easy to put it out of your mind, to ponder the dinner dilemma instead. You'll figure out something simple but delicious, without too much preparation. And ice cream for dessert.

You keep walking. You feel better. You're taking care of yourself and your family, and that's so important.

MAJESTY

THE KIDS ARE GROWING UP. I guess it was bound to happen eventually because that's how life works, haha. And Agamemnon is so tall! I can remember when he and Chloe were the same height, more or less, back when they met in Grade 2, and now the top of her head barely reaches his shoulders. It's cute.

He's very imposing. I've never seen a teenager with so many muscles! Last night he was wearing a crown that Chloe made for him out of construction paper, decorated with those little gem stickers I used to find stuck to everything in my house until she outgrew her crafting stage. But she must still have a secret stash somewhere. I never know with her these days.

We'd been up at the cottage and some of our friends were texting us to say they'd been hearing fireworks going off all weekend, so maybe they weren't even happening on the Monday this year. But I said no, this is Victoria Day. This is the day we celebrate, and we've always done it this way. It'll happen.

There are a few families who get together every year to buy the fireworks and then the dads set them off and we all sit on the hill and watch. It's tradition. And Agamemnon's dad has always been the one in charge. But this year, he stood back and let his son take over. And despite everything that happened because of it, I still think it was a good decision. At a certain point, you have to give your kids a certain amount of responsibility, or else they'll never succeed in life.

We drove home on Monday afternoon, which we would've done anyway to beat the traffic, and the second we pulled into our driveway, Chloe was out of the car and sprinting in her flip-flops down the street to Aggie's house, because of hormones and Young Love and all the reasons she can't stand to be around us these days. But it's fine. I can remember being fifteen and all I ever did was listen to the Cranberries and smoke menthol cigarettes and hate my parents. Honestly I was blown away when she agreed to come to the cottage without a fight, but if we didn't have wifi, I'm sure it would've been a different story.

Jim and I unpacked the car and made popcorn and grabbed our picnic blanket and a bottle of wine and we headed for the hill. In the winter, everyone toboggans there and you'd think eventually the grass wouldn't grow back. But it does, every spring. Greener than ever.

I will admit that things did get a bit wild with Agamemnon in charge. There wasn't the sense of control you felt when the adults were doing it. About fifteen minutes in, the first firework fell over after it was lit and went sideways instead of up. It hit the side of the hill, which was unsettling. But not dangerous. It was careless, I'd call it, rather than reckless, like some people are saying.

But nobody was going to argue about the quality of the show itself. All the little kids around us were oohing and aahing and clinging to their parents and I thought back to when Chloe used to be that size and how she used to sit in my lap during the fireworks, and we'd snuggle together on the picnic blanket and eat popcorn.

And they weren't being careless *on purpose*, that much was obvious to me. It was because they were all filming it with their phones, streaming it or posting it or whatever they do, so they were distracted, that's all. Their focus was elsewhere. The dads probably should've stepped in at some point. But they didn't, and here we are.

There were actually a couple groups of teenagers setting off fireworks on both sides of the crowd, which was something new. In the past, you might see a handful of inconsequential explosions going off in the north side of the park on the soccer field, whereas the bulk of the show was always concentrated in the south side on the baseball diamond at the bottom of the hill. But this time there were two exuberant displays going on, north and south, almost simultaneously. Like a competition. And both presentations were equally impressive. The vibrant colours and thrilling effects of light and sound were dazzling. There was so much MAJESTY.

If you asked me to pick the clear winner, I would say Aggie's team was the best. But of course I'm biased. We just adore that boy. We had him over for dinner last week and he said to me, "Jaclyn, you make good pie." And I told him I'd bought the pie at the Superstore, and we all laughed so hard. Even Chloe. And then the two of them disappeared into the night to do whatever it is they do.

We used to be more connected. Chloe and I. But between ballet and tutoring and basketball and gymnastics and dance and farm camp and the arts and crafts classes, Jim and I didn't see much of her when she was growing up. But we went as a family to the fireworks on the hill every Victoria Day, and we enjoyed it. Those are memories that I'll always treasure, and that I won't allow to be tainted by what happened this year. Because it wasn't even that bad, really. It was just a bunch of kids being kids.

It never got so bad that we considered calling the police. Who wants to call the cops on your neighbours' kids? It was loud, yes, but it's always loud. You know that going in. It's fireworks! You can wear earplugs if you don't like the noise. Some of the littlest kids got scared, but that's always the case. Once they start screaming, that means it's bedtime. No big deal.

It was also reassuring to see a few familiar white-haired dads from the original fireworks families hovering with their beers in the background. Surely they'd given their sons a few tips ahead of time, a safety lesson. Some warnings maybe about misuse and all that. But that's all you can do. At a certain point, you need to let go and let them find their own way. You can send the message, but you can't control how that message is received. Otherwise they'll never learn.

As far back as I can remember, and we've lived here a long time, these good folks get together year after year and put on this event, which is always just as spectacular—if not more so—than anything professional you'd experience anywhere else in the city. They spend thousands of dollars to entertain the whole neighbourhood. So what if the dads eventually got tired of doing the actual physical work of it and wanted to pass the torch. Everyone just needs to stop with the disparaging comments and be grateful for once.

There was also some hesitation to call the police because several of us had already been calling them about the man in the park. All this time we've been lucky, but then he showed up. He didn't even have a tent! At least with a tent he could've had a place to put his things, instead of just flinging them all around the tree he decided to claim.

This is our park. We have roots in this neighbourhood. We moved here and our kid grew up here. But suddenly there was this man and we felt unsafe. How is that fair?

Some people felt badly for him, and of course I did too. Then some people started bringing him food, which only encouraged him to stay. But he needed to go. There are laws against camping in the park. It's illegal, plain and simple. You can't do it.

Now there are people on social media who are saying that our neighbourhood is "too white." Give me a break. That has absolutely nothing to do with it.

First of all, I'm pretty sure Agamemnon's family is Greek. And secondly, those people might change their tune if they knew that the student council at Aggie and Chloe's high school organized two anti-racist evenings in the last year.

Both events were on Zoom, which made things feel a bit more impersonal, but I like that I can turn off my camera if I want to. One of the events was called "How to Talk About Racism with Your (White) Teens." It bothered me that the "white" was in parentheses. I understand that the conversation is different somehow when your child isn't white. Because they already know about racism is the implication, whereas with white children, they're suggesting, it's something totally new and unfathomable that has to be explained. Which to me rings a wee bit judgmental. As if none of the white parents have ever talked to their kids about this very serious issue. Like, give us SOME credit, you know? At least a dozen moms, if not a few more than that, showed up to this event signalling our commitment to the cause, but without those parentheses in the description, there might've been a lot more. The parentheses were off-putting, I won't lie.

The other event was called "My Racism Journey." There were only five of us at that one, but to be fair, there were a lot of big tournaments going on that night. Football and soccer and also chess, if I'm not mistaken. There were two presenters, a young woman and a young man, both of colour, who talked to us about examples of the racism they had experienced in their lives. None of the incidents they described were particularly dramatic or upsetting, but we all paid polite attention and gave them the benefit of the doubt. And for sure, it made sense that all the things they told us about, even though on their own they didn't sound too bad, felt worse when they were all added together.

About halfway through that presentation, the young woman, who had very cool hair, put up a slide that read, "My ANTI-Racism Journey." And we all went, "Aha!" It was kind of uplifting, this moment of recognition that we all shared. Like, *Of course! Let's STOP learning about racism and START learning about anti-racism!*

I can't remember much after that, except for the part where they asked us to reflect on a time in our lives when we knew we were thinking a racist thought but we thought it anyway.

For me it was last month, when we were in Florida. Chloe and I wanted to go to a Michelin-starred restaurant, but it was too far to walk, and Jim had to work, so he installed the Lyft app on my phone. And when the app showed me who our driver would be, I got nervous.

Yes, he was Black. But he was also a man.

That's why I was nervous. He could've been any colour of man. The honest truth is that we've been living through COVID for more than two years, and all that time we'd been driving everywhere—no cabs, definitely no public transportation—and I was anxious about getting into a vehicle with a stranger. I especially didn't feel comfortable being alone with my teenage daughter, both of us dressed up for an outing to a nice restaurant, in a car with a strange man. It didn't matter what he looked like. When his profile appeared on my phone, my first thought was, *Okay, it's a man.* I'd been hoping for a woman.

And when he didn't pull up to the hotel, I'll admit I was relieved. The app said he'd arrived, but clearly something had gone wrong. And when my phone rang and I didn't recognize the number, I figured that it was probably him, but I didn't answer it because by then I didn't even want to go to that restaurant. I just wanted to get takeout from the Steak 'n Shake across the road from our hotel and eat it in our suite watching the second season of *Love Is Blind*. And Chloe felt the same way, which was nice for a change.

Anyway, if I was aware of the possibility that I was being racist, I'm pretty sure that means I *wasn't* being racist.

And I did feel badly for the man in the park, but I definitely didn't feel comfortable engaging with him. He was clearly unstable, so who knew what could happen if I said hello and gave him some food. He might become obsessed with me and my family. From his spot under the big tree, he could see right into our house. He could've been watching us the whole time. It was difficult to tell where he was looking unless I used my binoculars, which I had to do very sparingly because I didn't want to inadvertently enrage him if he caught me doing that.

The park was so peaceful before he arrived. After he arrived, all we could see was him and his things all spread out everywhere.

I understand he was unwell. And maybe life wasn't kind to him. You wonder how that happens. You wonder how people get like that. But get out of our park.

By the time the second and third sets of fireworks went sideways into the hill, most of the youngest kids were gone already. A few parents carrying babies or toddlers started swearing at Aggie and his friends, but it's not as if we didn't have time to move out of the way. It did occur to me that maybe one of the misfires might've been on purpose. Not to hurt anybody, just to push the envelope a bit. Testing the limits, which is what teenagers naturally do. But probably they were all just accidents.

Anyhow, we were getting tired by then. The wine was finished and Jim was already folding up the blanket. We waved goodbye to Chloe, who was way down at the bottom of the hill with the rest of them, and I think she waved back.

We always made it a habit never to swear in front of her when she was little.

As Jim and I were leaving, there were a few minor bangs and flashes of light over by the big tree where the man had illegally set up camp. I heard shouting too, but then I heard laughter, so I assumed there was no harm done. Somebody said there was an altercation, but I couldn't really see anything because it was too dark. All I know is that the ambulance came and took the man away and he didn't come back.

When I woke up this morning, I opened the blinds on our front window and saw a crew of city employees in bright yellow jackets under the tree, all working hard together to clean up his mess. When they were done, they drove off in their bright white pickup truck. The park was pristine again, like the man had never been there at all. And I'll admit I was relieved.

Chloe told us she and Aggie weren't directly involved in whatever it was that happened, and we believe her. Jim actually called her late last night to ask if she'd recorded anything incriminating, and she said no. And really, from what we could tell, it was mostly just a few of the rowdier kids chasing each other with fireworks—the smaller and less expensive ones—far away from the spectators. Nothing serious. The occasional loud *pop* and then a burst of red or green. That's all it was.

But like I said, Jim and I were on our way home at that point, just to be safe. Even though I'm convinced there was never really anything for us to worry about.

CHERYL, ARE YOU OKAY?

CHERYL, I AM FEELING THIS ENORMOUS PRESSURE that is filling me up inside.

Cheryl, this feeling does not feel good. It's something new and it's been building and building inside me, and before I felt it, I felt nothing at all. There was only harmony. Now it's all disharmony.

Cheryl, I saw you out walking the other day at lunch and I waved to you but I think you didn't see me. I wanted to tell you something that day but I wasn't quite sure how to articulate it, but now I think I can.

This pressure just keeps building and it's like, do you know when you have to let something out but it's stuck really deep inside? And the thing inside you is so big that you start to become afraid it might never come out, and it will be stuck deep inside you creating that unbearable feeling of pressure forever?

I would compare it to giving birth maybe, but I had a C-section.

Do you know that some women in my life have told me that because I had a C-section, that means I'm less of a mother? Yes, Cheryl, there are women who have actually said that to my face. It used to hurt my feelings but then I stopped caring what they said and what they thought.

When I was in labour I did try pushing for a while, but it didn't work. I kept yelling at the nurse, "The book said I'm supposed to feel an irresistible urge to bear down! Where is my irresistible urge to bear down?" But Olivia just wasn't coming out of me that way. So eventually they said, "Sorry,

Beth-Ann, we have to do it another way." And I wondered why they were apologizing, because to me in that moment, getting a C-section was the same as winning the lottery. *Vaginal-delivery bullet dodged!* I thought, because to be honest I was terrified all along of getting ripped open at the end.

Cheryl, please help me remove this unbearable feeling.

Cheryl, do you know how I figured out about lived experience? It was way back at the start of #MeToo. I was trying to explain to my husband how it feels to be a woman who finds herself alone somewhere with a strange man—in a taxi, in an elevator, in a parking garage, on a subway train, in a park at night, or in any number of endless similar situations that we're all familiar with—and he could not even come close to comprehending what that fear feels like. Although I could see him trying and I appreciated that.

And then I heard about Black Lives Matter.

And then you got hired, and I remembered that conversation with my husband and it felt significant somehow.

I am trying, Cheryl. But I know my limits. I know I can't ever step into your shoes. Which is why I'm asking you to explain it to me. Like how I helped my husband try to view the world through female eyes. And that conversation brought us closer, because it was like suddenly a light went on for him, and after that he started doing the dishes more often without even needing to be asked.

Cheryl, I read an article that said the pink hats are offensive because they exclude certain people so I'm not going to wear mine anymore. I only wore it to the marches because I thought it was cute and because the marches happened in the winter and it was freezing.

The other day when you were out walking at lunch and didn't see me waving, you were wearing a bright turquoise hat that perfectly complemented your ebony complexion, which made me acutely aware of my own lack of colour. My dullness, even.

Cheryl, your advice is the advice that I need. It has only recently occurred to me how little I know and understand. And you know so much! Remember last summer, when I invited you to my cottage but you were unavailable? I was going to ask for your advice then, but I couldn't.

But Cheryl, you know me. You know I am not the same as them. I know all sorts of people who often make inappropriate jokes or comments but I have never in my entire life made a joke or comment like that. Also I make a point of not laughing or even reacting when I hear those jokes or comments because I believe in equality. It's important to me that you know that. It's important to me that you know that I want to be better. I am learning but my learning can only take me so far.

Cheryl, I am wondering if you saw the petitions I have been posting on my Facebook page. I have been posting a lot of petitions lately. And I don't just post the petition, I also say something about it, to increase the likelihood that people will sign it.

Cheryl, I didn't grow up with any of this stuff. My parents never talked about it. My parents are good people but they were raised not to talk about things. And then as a result, so was I. Also I never really knew anyone else who isn't like me because I have always been surrounded by people like me. Isn't that odd? Now I'm thinking to myself, *Where were all those other people when I was growing up?*

So when I met you, I was so happy.

I'm serious, Cheryl. I am not making this up.

There was no one who was not like me on the street I grew up on, or at my elementary school. (No, but there was one Asian boy in my Grade 2 class! I am not sure if "Asian" is the correct term to use anymore? I overheard you and Tamara talking last week about how you both find it annoying that "Asian" is a food group at the supermarket, and I sort of understand why you would be annoyed at that but then no, I don't really understand at all.) Or at my high school or at my university or at any of the part-time jobs I ever had. Or anywhere during my post-university trip to Europe. Or anywhere during my post-European-trip carefree party days in my twenties when I moved out of my parents' house in the suburbs and found a little apartment in the city when I answered an ad in the Roommates Wanted section of the weekly paper. That makes me sound old, so you'd think I'd be wiser by now haha, but Cheryl, I'm not. And my friends and I went to so many bars and parties all the time in our twenties and our thirties where we danced and drank and whooped it up with more people like us, and then I met my husband and he was like me and all of his friends were also like us. And then I got my job, and before you and Tamara started, everybody was the same there too.

Okay wait, I guess if I stop and think about it, there were maybe some people in the background. In some stores and some restaurants, but mostly at the library and on public transit.

And then my husband and I bought our house and we had our daughter, and now she goes to a school where most of the kids and most of the parents are like us, so the same pattern is beginning all over again. It just goes on and on. Yes there are the nannies, but they mostly keep to themselves. (Our daughter is in daycare, Cheryl. I think I mentioned that to you once but I'm not sure if you'd remember.) It's strange how that happens, isn't it, that separation? We certainly never planned it that way. It's just the way it's always been. Why are our worlds so far apart? I find myself wondering that now.

Cheryl, I miss when you used to talk to me. When I would pass by your desk and say hello and you would say hello back to me, and sometimes we would talk about the weather or our favourite yogurt flavours or a funny Internet meme we'd both seen. Or sometimes we would chuckle about how tired we were. For a while I thought we were becoming friends. I told my husband about you. I told him how much I enjoyed our conversations at work. But then you stopped talking to me and I don't know why. I'm still trying to figure it out.

Is it because we never talked about our families? I don't even know if you're married. I never asked you personal questions because I didn't want to pry. But I heard Tamara telling you one time that her family is from Sri Lanka, and you were both smiling so much, and I can't remember where you told her your family is from so I should ask you, but Cheryl, I don't know how.

Are you married?

Cheryl, I did an interesting thing once. Way before you started working there, a perception expert came to the office and did a workshop with all the employees because management was unhappy with our creativity ratios. The goal was for us to "become more mindful of how narrow our scope of awareness is by doing an exercise to encourage us to widen our lenses of consciousness." Those were the exact words the expert used. I can still clearly recall everything she said because that workshop really affected me.

The expert told us some things and then she sent us outside for our lunch break, and as we left the conference room, she handed each of us a folded-up piece of paper. "This is your colour," she said. "Hold on to it. Do not unfold this piece of paper until you get outside. Make sure you're alone when you read the word. Then close your eyes. Then open them again."

So I took my folded-up piece of paper and carried it outside and I went to my favourite spot behind the building that I haven't shown you yet, but I would like to show you one day. Or maybe you already know about it. There is a bench that is always empty, next to a planter that used to have flowers in it but then the flowers died and nobody replaced them. So there is only dirt inside the planter now.

When the weather is pleasant, like it was that day, I like to sit on that bench by myself and eat my lunch. And when I'm done eating, I like to put my hands into that cool soil and pretend that my fingers are the long, grasping roots of plants. Or sometimes I wriggle my fingers like earthworms. I know that's bizarre. It's just a thing I like to do. It makes me feel better.

That day when we had the workshop, I sat on the bench and I was so eager to unfold my paper that I ripped it a little, and then I was sitting there as still as a statue with nobody else around and I was silently looking at my word that seemed to pulsate on the page: BLUE.

Then I closed my eyes as we had been instructed to, and then I opened them again.

And Cheryl, the effect was instantaneous. It was like a magic trick.

All of a sudden, all the other colours had disappeared and blue was all I could see. There was nothing else. My gaze jumped from one blue thing to another: the recycling bin beside me, the faded lettering on the wall behind me that must've always been there but I'd never registered it until that moment. A thin strip of paint extending along the top of the bench that I'd never noticed before. A bird! A plastic bag caught in a tree! My pants! And the sky, of course. I won't even attempt to describe the intensity and saturation of blue in the sky that day. There might've been a few clouds, I'm not sure. It doesn't matter.

Cheryl, I have never experienced anything quite like that before, and I don't think I ever will again. The feeling of being surrounded and overwhelmed by all that blue. It was life-changing. And I think it's connected to this discussion in some way but I have no idea how, so I was hoping you might have some insight you could offer?

Cheryl, are you okay? I saw that thing on the news. It was horrible. I thought of you right away. I'm still thinking of you. I can't imagine. It's awful, Cheryl. My heart goes out to you. My heart is flying toward you at top speed. My heart is reaching for your heart across a vast, immeasurable distance. I really hope you are doing okay. I hope the darkness does not extinguish your light. I hope you are still finding joy. I am hopeful that if we combine our light, there will be no more terrible things.

Those awful things are in the news too much and the other day I overheard you telling Tamara you were sad and l know I can't feel your pain as if it's my own, but I'm trying to. Just tell me what to do. Tell me how I can help. Help me out, Cheryl. I see you. I hear you. I'm with you. I stand by you. I don't know what else I can do.

I wore the safety pin and then I took it off when my cousin posted something about the safety pin not being helpful, that it actually might be co-opted by people with bad intentions instead of good ones. Cheryl, I put up the black square. I'm not sure if you saw it. I put it up on that day we were supposed to and then I left it up for a few days longer before I read a post from my cousin saying that the black square was not helpful although she didn't say why, but in any case I took it down immediately. I added the rainbow filter to my profile picture on the day we were supposed to and I don't think there was anything wrong with that one, was there? I retweeted some things I thought might be helpful. I am using my platform to amplify voices.

I am doing all of those things but I know there are more things I could be doing but I don't know what those things are.

Cheryl, we are exploring new territory in my book club. As of next month we will be prioritizing BIPOC and LGBTQ+ and disabled stories. Does the content of the stories matter? Should the books be about specific issues? We're unclear about that. We like thrillers and we like stories about characters who embark on quests, but we are totally willing to set those preferences aside if need be.

We are opening up, Cheryl. The other week my cousin posted an article about how to be an ally and I shared it with the book-club gals and they all thought it was great, and as a result we have started to acknowledge our whiteness and our privilege and our fragility and our complicity with each other. It's all out there for everyone to see now.

Cheryl, I'm embarrassed to admit that occasionally I have trouble telling people of different backgrounds apart. But once in a while I will get one white person mixed up with another white person, so maybe I'm just bad at recognizing faces? I always know who *you* are, though!

Except for that one time, when you and Tamara were both wearing really similar green pantsuits.

I'm so sorry about that time.

Cheryl, I am aware that I get an overly wide and unnatural smile whenever I encounter certain people in public places. Cheryl, I don't know how to not do that smile. I'm trying but it just pops onto my face.

Cheryl, I can tell you are suffering and I don't want to minimize that.

I can tell there is something going on with you and I feel so far away from you, Cheryl, but I don't want to be so far away. You are over there and I am over here, and the other day when I saw you out walking at lunch, I thought about trying to catch up to you and asking how you were doing, but you were walking so fast so I couldn't.

I admire you, Cheryl. You are beautiful and strong. And Tamara is beautiful and strong. I have so much admiration for both of you and I want you to know that, but I don't know how to say it in a way that doesn't sound weird.

Cheryl, I am not okay. But I am starting to realize that maybe there are different levels of not being okay that do not apply equally to all of us. Maybe "levels" is not the right word?

Cheryl, maybe I shouldn't send you this letter.

Maybe I'll just hold on to it for now.

ACKNOWLEDGEMENTS

I'm very grateful for the financial support I received for this collection from the Canada Council for the Arts' Research and Creation Component of the Explore and Create program, from the Ontario Arts Council's Literary Creation Projects (Works for Publication) program, and from the Ontario Arts Council's Recommender Grants for Writers program (many thanks to Biblioasis, Inanna Publications and Education Inc., Invisible Publishing, *Taddle Creek*, and *The New Quarterly* for recommending my work).

Thank you to the readers. Thank you to the librarians. Thank you to the booksellers (especially the glorious indies).

To Bryan Ibeas, editor of my dreams: I was beyond thrilled for the chance to collaborate with you again. Thank you for your super-incisive edits and empowering suggestions and our conversations that lit up my brain, and for helping me get this book to exactly where I wanted it to be. Your belief in my work means the world to me.

To Brittany Chung Campbell: Thank you for your invaluable sensitivity reading of my manuscript. Your generous and insightful feedback enabled me to add layers of depth and meaning to my stories that I wouldn't have considered without your guidance and encouragement. It was such a joy to work with you.

To Norm Nehmetallah, publisher extraordinaire: From the very first time we met, I was buoyed by your warmth, enthusiasm, and dedication. My sincere thanks for the immense care and thought you have given me and this book.

To Jules Wilson: It was excellent to be in your orbit again. Thank you so much for your stellar and wholehearted publicity work and your cheering-on.

To Megan Fildes: Thank you for creating the most stunning cover art I could have imagined. It makes me giddy every time I look at it. Thanks also for your typesetting magic.

To Stuart Ross: It made me so happy that you were the copy editor! Thank you for trusting my words, for your meticulous reading, and for your spot-on edits and fantastic catches.

To Brock Peters: Many thanks for your careful proofreading.

To Alicia Elliott: Thank you so much for your thoughtful sensitivity reading of "Pioneers," and for your perceptive editorial suggestions that allowed me to clarify the intention of this story.

To Tamanna Bhasin: Thank you for your vital sensitivity reading of earlier drafts of "Swimming Lesson," "A Warm and Lighthearted Feeling," "Gary How Does a Contact Form Work?" and "Avalanche." Your thoughtful and detailed feedback informed so much of this collection.

To Sam Hiyate, literary agent of amazingness: Thank you, as always, for your unflagging excitement about my writing and for all that you do.

To the brilliant first readers of my manuscript in various drafts: Your insight was absolutely indispensable. I'm so grateful for the time and care you so generously gave me and this book. My heartfelt thanks to: Jami Heydari, Caroline Habib,

Greg Kearney, Kate Barton, Amy Miranda, and Carrianne Leung. With a special thank you to Carrianne for our conversation on that sunny, chilly day in Grange Park, which helped me immeasurably to understand what I wanted this collection to do.

To the marvelous first readers of various stories at various times: The thoughts you shared helped to light my way. Many thanks to: Ali Lamontagne, Brittan Coghlin Ullrich, Teri Vlassopoulos, Kelli Deeth, Shannon Alberta, Sara Heinonen, Grace O'Connell, Kate Zieman, Nicole Knibb, Neil Smith, and Casey Plett. With a special thank you to Casey for your kindness and advice during that early pandemic phone-beer chat.

To my friends and colleagues for their generous words of encouragement about "Gary How Does a Contact Form Work?" that heartened me more than I can say: Kwame Scott Fraser, Samantha Garner, Teri Vlassopoulos, Kelvin Kong, Gavin Barrett, Mayank Bhatt, and Sonal Champsee.

Thank you to Bianca Spence for that long-ago conversation over beers at the Prenup Pub that still shines so brightly for me, and for introducing me to the megaphone.

Thank you to Whitney French for our meandering and inspiring phone chats that have enlarged my sense of what is possible.

For our conversations about the ideas inside these stories, thank you to Jasmine Macaulay, Alison Kearns, Kelli Deeth, Nicole Knibb, Cynthia Welton, Brittan Coghlin Ullrich, Jen Noble, Shannon Alberta, and Jenna Bly. And for helping me figure some important things out, thank you to Dorianne Emmerton and Jim Munroe.

Thank you to my parents, Linda and Tim Westhead, for story-reading and for your endless love and support. To my brother, Cameron Westhead, for our conversation about a story that meant so much to me, and to you and Marcella for cheering me on. To Jane and Klaus and Jason Wuenschirs for your love and support. To my (great!) Aunt Lori Barton, for all of your love and encouragement. To my cousins Don McKellar and Kate Barton for always being in my corner. With a special thank you to Kate for your dearly appreciated perspective and our conversations that have helped to shape how I want to be in the world.

The following books were pivotal in helping me organize my thoughts about this collection, and I'm very grateful to their authors: *A Mind Spread Out on the Ground* by Alicia Elliott, *Black Writers Matter* edited by Whitney French, *So You Want to Talk About Race* by Ijeoma Oluo, *What White People Can Do Next: From Allyship to Coalition* by Emma Dabiri, *Nice White Ladies: The Truth about White Supremacy, Our Role in It, and How We Can Help Dismantle It* by Jessie Daniels, and *White Women: Everything You Already Know About Your Own Racism and How to Do Better* by Regina Jackson and Saira Rao. Many thanks also to the writers with the On Canada Project, whose work has illuminated so much for me.

And to my two favourite people in the entire universe and beyond: Thank you to Derek and Luisa Wuenschirs for your hugs that make everything better, for making me laugh my embarrassing laugh, and for just generally being the most wonderful company imaginable. I love you both so very much.

NOTES

Earlier drafts of some of the stories in this book appeared in the following publications:

A previous version of "Swimming Lesson" was published in *Joyland*.

A previous version of "Something Fun to Do on a Beautiful Day" was published in *The New Quarterly*.

A previous version of "This Is the Way" was published in *Taddle Creek*.

A previous version of "Gary How Does a Contact Form Work Do I Just Type in Here and Then Press Send and That's It?" was published in *The Ampersand Review*.

Thank you to those editors for the care and attention they gave to my work.

ABOUT THE AUTHOR

Jessica Westhead is the author of the novels *Pulpy & Midge* (Coach House Books) and *Worry* (HarperCollins Canada), and the short story collections *And Also Sharks* and *Things Not to Do* (Cormorant Books). *And Also Sharks* was a *Globe & Mail* Top 100 Book, one of Kobo's Best Ebooks of 2011, and a finalist for the Danuta Gleed Short Fiction Prize, and *Worry* was included on CBC Books' Best Canadian Fiction of 2019 and the CBC Canada Reads Longlist. Jessica has taught creative writing at The G. Raymond Chang School of Continuing Education at Toronto Metropolitan University, and the School of Continuing Studies at the University of Toronto. She lives in Toronto with her family.

INVISIBLE PUBLISHING produces fine Canadian literature for those who enjoy such things. As an independent, not-for-profit publisher, we work to build communities that sustain and encourage engaging, literary, and current writing.

Invisible Publishing has been in operation for over a decade. We released our first fiction titles in the spring of 2007, and our catalogue has come to include works of graphic fiction and nonfiction, pop culture biographies, experimental poetry, and prose.

We are committed to publishing writers with diverse perspectives. In acknowledging historical and systemic barriers, and the limits of our existing catalogue, we emphatically encourage writers from LGBTQ2SIA+ communities, Indigenous writers, and writers of colour to submit their work.

Invisible Publishing is also home to the Bibliophonic series of music books and the Throwback series of CanLit reissues.

If you'd like to know more, please get
in touch: info@invisiblepublishing.com

Invisible